Full
Circle

By:

Brooke St. James

No part of this book may be used or reproduced in any form or by any means without prior written permission of the author.

So This is Love (Miami Stories #1)
All In (Miami Stories #2)
Something Precious (Miami Stories #3)

The Suite Life (The Family Stone #1)
Feels Like Forever (The Family Stone #2)
Treat You Better (The Family Stone #3)
The Sweetheart of Summer Street (The Family Stone #4)
Out of Nowhere (The Family Stone #5)

Delicate Balance (Blair Brothers #1)
Cherished (Blair Brothers #2)
The Whole Story (Blair Brothers #3)
Dream Chaser (Blair Brothers #4)

Kiss & Tell (Novella) (Tanner Family #0)
Mischief & Mayhem (Tanner Family #1
Reckless & Wild (Tanner Family #2)
Heart & Soul (Tanner Family #3)
Me & Mister Everything (Tanner Family #4)
Through & Through (Tanner Family #5)
Lost & Found (Tanner Family #6)
Sparks & Embers (Tanner Family #7)
Young & Wild (Tanner Family #8)

Easy Does It (Bank Street Stories #1)
The Trouble with Crushes (Bank Street Stories #2)
A King for Christmas (Novella) (A Bank Street Christmas)
Diamonds Are Forever (Bank Street Stories #3)
Secret Rooms and Stolen Kisses (Bank Street Stories #4)
Feels Like Home (Bank Street Stories #5)
Just Like Romeo and Juliet (Bank Street Stories #6)
See You in Seattle (Bank Street Stories #7)
The Sweetest Thing (Bank Street Stories #8)
Back to Bank Street (Bank Street Stories #9)

Split Decision (How to Tame a Heartbreaker #1)
B-Side (How to Tame a Heartbreaker #2)

Cole for Christmas

Somewhere in Seattle (Alexander Family #1)
Wildest Dream (Alexander Family #2)
About to Fall (Alexander Family #3)

Hope for the Best (Morgan Family #1)
Full Circle (Morgan Family #2)

Chapter 1

Lila Morgan
***
Houston, Texas

I was fifteen minutes late.

This was not a good way for me to start things off. At least I wasn't late for my *actual* meeting—I was only late for my pre-meeting meeting, the one I had scheduled with my brother.

I let out a resolute sigh as I checked the time, stuffed my phone into my purse, and continued down the busy sidewalk in Downtown Houston. I never came to this part of the city. I lived and worked in the suburbs north of Houston, and I rarely came downtown. Hence the reason I was late. I had underestimated the traffic by fifteen minutes.

I opened the door to the coffee shop, and the cold January air was met with wonderful warm air that smelled like fresh-brewed coffee. The room was full of sights, sounds, and scents. I spotted my brother right away in spite of the fact that it was crowded in there. Beck was in the next room, and I could see him sitting at a table by himself.

The atmosphere in Wesley's Coffee was amazing, and I smiled and straightened my shoulders. It might have been my favorite coffee shop in the whole world. As far as I knew, there were only two locations, the newer one in Woodland Hills and this one, the original. I had never been to this one, and it was even cooler than the one near my house.

The music was louder in Wesley's than it was in a regular coffee shop, and that fact alone changed the vibe. I didn't recognize the song, but they were playing some slow and easy alternative rock that made me feel like a cool person. I felt like it was my personal soundtrack as I walked in.

I grinned and headed toward my brother. He turned and caught sight of me, waving me over, and I continued walking that way.

"I already got our drinks," he called as I came closer.

It was packed in there, and I could see a guy sitting at the table next to my brother. I glanced at the side of his face as I walked up. He was a young man, and he was comfortably propped in the booth that was just a couple of feet from my brother. The man didn't have anyone there with him, but he was sprawled out, occupying the whole booth. There was a backpack, a tablet, and several other things on the table.

I only noticed how comfortable he looked because of how cramped my brother and I were.

There were what must have been six people on the other side of us, and they were all stuffed into a table for four, crowding us. Our little table was right next to the single guy, and I did my best to avoid bumping into him as my brother stood to greet me.

"Sorry I'm late," I said, hugging my brother.

"It's fine. I knew you would be, that's why I told you we should meet here before your interview."

"Thank you for doing that. I would be panicking right now if I was late for my meeting. You saved me. It's January. It's forty degrees out there, and I'm so nervous that my pits are sweating. Thank goodness I wore black. Thank you for getting my drink."

I was only so candid because the single guy had on earbuds and the group at the other table was so loud that there was no way I could be heard.

I switched places with my brother so that I could sit in the chair opposite him. I glanced at the guy again as I made it over there. He was positioned next to my brother, so I could see him clearly. He glanced at me, and he was so handsome that I felt stunned. I regretted the comment about my underarms, and I was thankful he had earbuds in his ears. He gave me a quick, absentminded grin before going back to whatever he was doing in his leather portfolio.

I wondered if he was writing or drawing. His relaxed posture made me think he was drawing something, but I couldn't be sure since I couldn't see what it was on his notepad.

I did not give myself time to think about it. I took my eyes off of the stranger and inspected my brother, Beck's, appearance instead. He still had on a jacket though it was warm inside. He was dressed in dark, stylish but broken-in clothing. He was a successful visual artist, a painter, and he hung out with artistic types. He always looked nice and he pulled it off in a way that looked like he hadn't put any effort into it.

"I like your jacket," I said.

"Thank you."

"What coffee did you get me?"

"I got you a latte. Hazelnut. It's probably barely warm by now."

"It's okay, It's better that way with my sweat situation." I took off my jacket and used my hands to unapologetically fan my face and then my armpits, making a silly face at my brother.

He laughed, and the stranger across from me shot a quick glance in my direction and caught me fanning, so I stopped immediately. I sat up and took a sip of the coffee like I was a proper lady.

"It's good, thank you," I said.

I could see from my periphery that the stranger had gone back to what he was doing on the notepad. He was completely distracted, and his fingers drummed to a beat on the back of it. I knew his music had to be loud to drown out the music in the coffee shop.

"What are you doing at this meeting?" my brother asked.

"I'm talking to Frank Quinn."

"I know that, but what are you doing?" Beck asked. "Do you have to audition for him today? Is that what this is about?"

"I don't know. If he wants me to read for a part, I will. I'm prepared to. He can just wave a wand and let me be an extra, but I'd rather not be an extra. I hope it's an audition."

"You need to be on your guard. People get taken advantage of all the time when they want to get famous. Show business is known for that."

"I don't want to get famous. I seriously want to act. I want to find a role I can study and conquer."

"Either way, you want an acting job and the guy upstairs can give it to you. Don't let him be sketchy with you."

"Are you saying that he would try to take advantage of me personally? Physically?"

Beck shrugged. "You never know these days. You have to be ready for anything."

I laughed and shook my head.

"What?"

"You're paranoid, Beck. This guy is a hundred years old."

Beck chuckled at me before his face turned serious. "Seriously, though, do you want me to go up there with you?"

"No. He was dad's patient at the hospital. I doubt he's going to be hitting on me if that's what you're implying."

"Just know those types of situations still exist. Does dad know him well? Was he okay with you going to his office by yourself?"

"Yes, Beck, it's fine. He's a big-time television producer. You don't get to be a producer with a fancy office when you're sketchy."

Beck made an exaggerated facial expression and stared at me. "Rich and famous people are weird all the time, Lila. You can't be intimidated by him. Why can't you talk to Uncle Danny? He's a movie producer. Be in one of his movies."

"I have talked to him. I mentioned it at the lake house the last time we were there. I said that I want to act. He didn't respond by offering to help, and honestly, I don't know that I would want him to. I need to try something on my own. I already feel bad enough that dad is hooking this meeting up. I would feel even worse if I got a job straight from my uncle."

"Are you going to have to move to Hollywood?" Beck asked.

"I don't know what to expect, honestly. He's mainly known for General Hospital, which is filmed there, but I think he has influence with other television shows."

"Why does he live here?"

"Because he's retired now. He's from Houston. His family still lives here. They're old money. I think they own this whole building. How far is your new studio from here?" I added.

"I can't believe you haven't been there yet," he said, shaking his head.

I squinted at him. "You've only been in it for two days. And I just finished the play."

"It's only a little over a mile from here, but it took me fifteen minutes," Beck said. "I could have walked."

"How do you like your new space? How's it coming together?"

"I love it. You need to come by."

"I will now that the play's over."

"It was *sooo* good," he said.

"I loved it," I said as I took another sip of my coffee. "I love acting, Beck."

He laughed.

"What?"

"I'm just thinking about Mom and Dad with both of us being artists. Poor Dad."

I let out a humorless laugh and Beck squinted at me like he was about to say something.

"Ooh, hang on," he said, switching gears. He leaned to the side and fished in his pocket, coming up with his phone and looking at it curiously. "It was buzzing in my pocket," Beck explained. "Hang on. It's my roommate. I need to answer this question. He's looking for something at the house."

Beck trailed off as he focused intently on his phone, and I began to glance around. The first place my eyes roamed was to the guy sitting next to my brother—the one who was alone.

It was almost as if he knew I had looked at him. He was not looking at me when I first glanced at him, but suddenly, he peered up and his eyes met mine.

I looked away, but I was just nervous and feisty enough to instantly glance back at him.

His eyes were still locked on mine.

They were dark.

He was dark. He was mysterious.

He had on a hoodie and he was sitting with his notepad propped in front of him. He just sat there and stared straight at me like it was the most normal thing in the world to do.

I did what anybody would do.

I stared back.

My eyes stayed locked on his.

His earbuds were still in place, but I could no longer see his fingers tapping. All I could see were his eyes. I wasn't going to blink first, and I wasn't going to flinch first. He was a good-looking man, and we sat there, staring at each other for a length of time that seemed surreal. I would have never done this under normal circumstances.

But I was about to go upstairs to an audition for a soap opera…

Maybe I was getting into character.

Maybe I was doing something whimsical like falling in love from across a table.

We blinked, but neither I nor the mystery man looked away. *What on earth were we doing?*

I watched as one corner of his mouth rose in a slow, easy smile. I couldn't see his entire face, but I saw enough to read his expression. *What was his expression, anyway? Was he flirting with me?* I could not tell. He might have just been smiling at the fact that we just stared at each other for an awkwardly long amount of time.

My brother's voice stirred me from my trance. "That was Topher. I swear, that guy would lose his head if it wasn't screwed on. He locked himself out and couldn't remember where the spare key is." My brother trailed off because he caught me looking at the guy and he turned to quickly inspect my area of interest. I was regarding my brother by the time he turned back to face me.

Chapter 2

I stayed at the coffee shop for another ten minutes with my brother. I was amped about my meeting, and while we were there, I asked Beck to talk me through some possible scenarios… some possible questions that could come up. I had no idea who Frank Quinn was looking to cast me as, and I had already prepared myself for most acting scenarios that appeared on the show.

My dad was Chief of Surgery at Houston's largest hospital. He was a powerful man of influence, and he was hard on us, his children. It was a testament to the sheer tenacity of myself and my brother that we both rebelled against him and chose to pursue artistic endeavors. My father didn't take it that well, but he had raised us to be too strong-willed to care.

Don Morgan was the type of guy who always seemed to have everything under control. Once, when I was a little girl, my father told me that he was only nervous for something if he wasn't prepared. I hated being nervous, and I had taken his advice seriously. I had been studying for this interview for a long time.

I might not have chosen to pursue a dream my father loved, but he respected my ambition and drive, and he eventually warmed up to the idea of me being an actress in my youth.

I thought the meeting with Frank Quinn would have happened weeks ago, and I was overjoyed that it was finally here. He had gone through a health crisis that took him away from his office, and he had just recently come back. My dad had called in a favor for this meeting, and calling in favors was something my father took seriously. He knew quite a few powerful and famous people, and he tried not to ask them for things very often.

My dad had lectured me multiple times about being on time today and making a good impression on Mr. Quinn. I left the coffee shop with enough time to make my way up to his office with seven minutes to spare.

It was a fifteen-story building, and Frank's office was on the top floor. I rode the elevator up to the top, feeling like I was in a movie with all the futuristic décor and glass hallways.

I had grown up in this city and been into a lot of buildings, but this one was beautiful. And it had a different vibe because I knew there was an interview or audition waiting for me behind one of these doors.

I checked in with a secretary.

She was middle-aged and wore her hair in a short bob with bangs. She told me in a pleasant but no-nonsense tone that Mr. Quinn would be with me in ten minutes and asked me to have a seat in the waiting room.

I did as she asked.

I sat there for a moment, looking around.

I eventually decided to get out my phone to check the time. I had a text from a friend of mine named Nadine. She was one of the few people I still connected with from high school. We only talked once or twice a year now, but she checked in now and then. She was always talking about God and inviting me to church, and she also always wanted to know about my love life and tell me about hers. Those were the two things I could count on her to check in with me about.

Nadine:
How long did it take you to get over your breakup? Because it's been a month since Ben and I split up, and I'm still not right.

I knew I would be waiting there for a few more minutes, so I typed back.

Me:
You broke up with your boyfriend? You'll be fine. Ben wasn't the best you could do, anyway. You are better off. That'll sink in one day, even if it's not today. You got this!

I pressed send and saw that she instantly started typing. A text came in within seconds.

Nadine:

You're right. I got this. It just hurts. I think being cheated on is worse than a regular breakup. How have you been? Any new guys in your life? Maybe I can rebound through you.

I smiled as I typed a reply.

Me:

Not really, no new dudes. Other than I think I might have fallen in love with a stranger in the coffee shop just now. There was prolonged eye contact.

Nadine:
How prolonged?

Me:
A minute.

Nadine:
Felt like a minute, or an actual minute?

Me:
An actual minute. At least.

Nadine:
You're kidding. From across the room? Was he looking at you? Are you sure?

Me:
Yes. He was staring right at me. It was from across the table.

Nadine:
He sat at your table?

Me:
The one right next to us. I was there with Beck.

Nadine:
What happened? Did you talk to him?

Me:
Beck?

Nadine:
No, the guy.

Me:
No.

Nadine:
You walked away?

Me:
Yes, I'm not there anymore.

Nadine:

You stared at him for a minute straight and didn't talk to him at all?

Me:
Yes.

Nadine:
You swear it was a minute?

Me:
Yes. We locked eyes. I promise. It was no big deal though. I was just nervous. I have to go to a job interview in a second.

Nadine:
Okay. Good luck.

Me:
Thank you. And you got this with the breakup.

I hit send. I expected her to reply with a generic thank you, but it was at that moment that Frank Quinn's secretary called my name. I stuffed my phone into my purse and stood up with a smile.

She ushered me into a large office. It had windows covering one wall, and as I entered, I stared out at the cityscape. Soon, I turned and my eyes fell onto Frank Quinn who was sitting behind a gigantic, well-crafted desk.

I had seen pictures of him before, so I knew what to expect. He was an older man dressed in a suit, just like I pictured.

And I was a nervous wreck.

"Hello," I said, testing my voice and trying to remain calm. I cleared my throat. I had to remind myself that I had nothing to lose. If he hated me, I still got to go back to my normal life.

"Hello, Miss Morgan."

"Hello," I repeated before I could stop myself. "I'm happy to be here, thank you for having me."

I did the things my parents taught me. I stood up straight, I made eye contact with him, I smiled, and I reached out to shake his hand as I approached his desk.

He stood and smiled as he shook my hand.

"Your father saved my life," he said, smiling at me.

"I'm so glad he did," I returned. "He's good at that."

"He certainly is. Have a seat. Lila. Is that your name? Lila Morgan?"

"Yes sir, I have my packet right here if you'd like to see it—my headshots and everything. I didn't know if you wanted to do that now, or..." I trailed off, knowing I was in danger of starting to ramble. I lifted the thin folder I was holding.

"I'll see your headshots," he said, motioning for me to hand the folder to him.

Mr. Quinn took it from me and opened it. He even put on some glasses so that he could look at what was inside. I had done research about what to take with me on an audition. I kept it simple, but I added personal creative touches. He smiled patiently as he inspected the contents, and I took a minute to catch my breath and try to calm my nerves.

"I heard you were pre-med at Baylor."

"Yes, sir."

"And straight A's." He glanced at me and I smiled humbly.

"Also true," I said. "But I'm switching gears. I'm taking some time off to pursue acting. I figured if there's something you want to do in life, there's no time like the present."

Frank Quinn gave me a barely-there smile, studying me. "Your dad said you were as stubborn and boneheaded as you are smart."

I smiled back at him and took a deep breath, not sure of what to say to respond to that. "I'm determined, I'll tell you that. I haven't been acting long, but I've done a lot of research on your show, and I'm taking lessons. I just finished my second community theater play the other day. I was Penny in Hairspray. My first role was ensemble in Cinderella, but then I landed Penny during my second production. We just wrapped that up the other day."

I clamped my mouth shut. None of that was planned dialogue.

"Oh, yeah, and how did it go?" he asked, looking up from my packet.

"Penny, you mean? Hairspray? It was great. There's a ton of dancing in that show. Somebody's shoe flew off and hit me in the head during the middle of a scene, but other than that, it went great."

He laughed at that, and it was good to see him being lighthearted since my dad said he was a no-nonsense type of guy. His smile faded a second later, and he set down the folder along with his glasses.

"I can get you on at General," he said. "I don't know what your goals are with acting, but solely based on the fact that your dad worked so hard to keep me alive, I can get you a job right out of the gate—a nurse role—something small at first." He took a deep breath and leveled me with a stare. "I'll be honest with you, though, Lila, I don't want to see you go out to LA. You'll either hate it and turn around and come back with your tail between your legs, or you'll love it, and you'll stay there. Either way, your daddy will hate me. But he assured me this is what you wanted."

It is, it is, it is.

"Yes sir, I'm excited and prepared. I would love the opportunity, and I'm extremely grateful for it, Mr. Quinn. Even a small role would be amazing. I feel like I could turn that into something bigger."

"I do have another proposition for you, Miss Morgan. Something you might not have thought about." He stared at me with a serious expression as he said it, and I thought of my brother and how he was being paranoid. I wondered if I should be paranoid, too. I thought of the mace in my purse. I glanced around for an exit route.

"What is it?" I asked hesitantly, feeling even more nervous than before.

"You wouldn't have to leave Houston for this. I know a young director who's making a movie and needs a female star. It would be a lead role, but it's his first movie. He may or may not be good at it—I can't make any promises for him. It's a risk you'll have to take. But if it were me, I'd stay here and try this role. If you're ready for a lead role."

"I'm ready for a lead role, but I don't do anything… immoral in my acting." I sounded so hesitant and regretful when I said it that I added, "I leave all my clothes on all the time."

He pulled back, staring at me with a surprised expression. "I hope you do, Miss Morgan. Your father wouldn't be too pleased with me if that weren't the case."

"I'm sorry. I just. I didn't know what you were… my brother was telling me to…" I trailed off with a sigh. "I'm sorry," I said, simply.

"I'm talking about a small, low-budget independent film. It's about a boy who witnessed a woman give birth. His nanny helped deliver the baby, and he watched the whole thing. It was one of his earliest memories. Then later, he ends up meeting up with the same girl—the baby who he saw being born."

"Oh, the three-year-old fell in love with the baby?" I asked, trying to understand.

"Yes, but not until later in life—when they're grown. I don't think they fall in love. They just meet. It's called Full Circle. I have the script right here. I read it, and it's not bad. Like I said, the director is new at this, and I can't vouch for his credibility. He's got a really small crew. But the script isn't bad."

Frank opened a desk drawer and pulled out a stack of paper that was about an inch thick. It was held together on the sides with three large clips. He slid it toward me. "Listen, take this and read it. There's no taking your clothes off or anything, but you might not even like it. You should feel a connection with the main character. The director assured me he'd make it good, but I am making no promises. Read it. If you love it and you want to play that lead, it's yours. If you don't want it, just drop the script off here at my office, and I'll make a phone call to California. You need to let me know by tomorrow, because he's already auditioned others for the role."

He wore a serious expression as he patted the script and pushed it again as if he wanted me to take it off of the desk.

"Do you think you can have it read by tomorrow at three o'clock?" he asked. "It's just a little ninety-minute film."

"I can definitely read it by then," I said. "Thank you for the opportunity."

"You're very welcome, Miss Morgan. Give your father my regards."

I agreed and stood up, picking up the script in the process. I almost said something about being sorry for questioning his intentions, but I didn't mention it. It was all fine and good, and we had settled the matter.

I held the stack of paper in my hands, feeling the thickness. A script. I might crack it open out of curiosity… but I was almost certain I was going to pass on the local gamble and go for greener pastures as an extra in Hollywood.

Chapter 3

Frank Quinn was not what I expected.

I thought that in my own mind as the elevator door closed and I began to ride downward.

First of all, he has no idea if I can act, and he never once asked me to prove whether or not I can. Secondly, a lead role with no audition? How good could the movie be?

I glanced downward at the thought, staring again at the stack of paper that I was holding—the script. I opened it and thumbed through it, feeling like I was in a dream.

A lead role in a movie? Maybe I can do it and then go to Hollywood. The movie would be a short-term time investment. I should've asked Frank Quinn how long the film was going to be in production. I should have asked him if I can do both.

I rode downward in the elevator, going back and forth about this new script and how I felt about it.

Suddenly, I felt my phone vibrating. I was in the middle of digging for it in my purse when the elevator door opened. I got off and moved to an area that was near the wall so that I could check my phone.

I had another text from Nadine, and I swiped the screen so that I could look at it. She normally didn't text me this often at all, and I squinted at the screen when I realized that two texts had come in from her. I read the first one.

Nadine:
I was thinking about the coffee shop guy, and I think you should go back over there.

Nadine:
I still keep thinking about it. Please go back to the coffee shop. It might be true love.

I grinned and laughed a little as I read the text, and then I put my phone in my purse and kept on walking. I felt a bit like I was in a hurry to go home and read the script even though I still wanted to move to Hollywood.

But then I walked by that coffee shop and there was nothing I could do to stop myself from going inside. The music playing was a classic rock song. It was epic, and the guy had a high-pitched voice. I was relatively sure it was Led Zeppelin. Again, I felt like a cool person, and I realized that was a nice side effect for a business. If I ever opened a business I would want people to feel cool when they walked in. I crossed to the area where we had been sitting a few moments ago.

The guy was still there. He was still sprawled out in the booth and concentrating on whatever he was working on. He was not facing me and had no idea I had come in.

Other people were now occupying our table, and it was busy in there, as usual.

I panicked internally, but on the outside, I just glanced around as if I was looking for something or someone. I hesitated, thinking about my options as the rock anthem played in the background.

There was no way I could walk over to him. What was I going to say? Hey, remember me? We stared at each other a minute ago? Good grief.

It wasn't like I could catch his eye from where I was standing. I would have to go up to him and tap him on the shoulder to get his attention.

I just couldn't make myself do it. I glanced around the place curiously and then I turned and went to the counter. I grabbed a granola bar from the display by the register and stood in line behind one other person.

It took me a few minutes to finish that transaction, and even by the end of it, I still couldn't work up the nerve to approach the guy from earlier. Nadine's hunch would have to go unfulfilled.

I left the coffee shop without looking back.

I didn't consider doing that movie at first, but as moments passed I grew more and more curious about the script. I went straight to my parent's house.

They had made me take over some bills and get a job when I switched my focus to acting and quit medical school, so I had been fitting in working a part-time administration job at my dad's hospital along with studying for roles and practicing my acting. I had my own apartment at their place, and I went in there without going to the main house first.

It was early afternoon, and I switched my professional attire for a messy bun with pajamas and slippers. I did the whole bit where I got myself a blanket and a few snacks before sitting down. I made a nice, comfortable, cozy spot on the couch.

It had been cold all day, and cloud cover had rolled in this afternoon, making it the perfect time for reading. My windows faced my parents' private, landscaped backyard, and I was about as relaxed as anyone could be. I sat back and lifted the script to get a good look at it.

The title page:

Full Circle

written by Wesley Quinn

At the bottom righthand side of the page were his email address and mailing address.

Wesley Quinn. My mind began putting pieces together about Wesley being related to Frank. I figured that was safe to assume since they shared the same last name. Oddly, though, Mr. Quinn had admitted that he didn't fully trust the director. Also, I couldn't understand why he would trust me to star in a movie with no experience or audition. I was conflicted about Full Circle already, and I hadn't even cracked it open.

I turned the page and began reading.

I sat on that couch and kept right on reading and reading until I was finished. I got up once to use the restroom, and I held the script with me and didn't stop reading the whole time.

I made a glass of water and drank it and I barely took my eyes off of the pages, even when I was eating, drinking, or walking. It took me four hours to get through it because I read slowly and tried to picture everything.

I.

Loved.

It.

The story began with a chance meeting between strangers, two young adults, Anna and Ben.

She had gotten into some trouble and was going upstate to live with an aunt. She was broke and had no hope in life.

Ben was the opposite of that. He had plenty of money, and it was his parents' money, so he hadn't worked for it. They were close in age, but they had completely different lifestyles and were an extremely unlikely pair.

Anna was waiting on a train out of town, and Ben was there picking someone up. I knew Anna was the main character right from the start, and my stomach was tied in knots the whole time I read because I imagined myself as her.

Much of the movie was dialogue between Anna and Ben, and there was an overwhelming amount of lines. They were good lines, though, and I smiled the whole time I read.

The two meet in a train station and begin talking on that bench, and the majority of the movie is their conversation, along with a series of flashbacks, as they sit there and talk about their own lives and experiences. They aren't romantic at all. They just laugh and reminisce about their own lives while they each have time to spare. They're natural and sarcastic together, and they get along as if they had known each other for years.

Then, toward the end, Ben starts describing this story that happened to him as a child.

He said it was his earliest memory ever.

He was with his nanny at the time, and she also happened to be a nurse. Ben's character narrates and tells this long story about this nanny and how she would try to give him real-life experiences since she knew he was living a fortunate, sheltered life. One day, she took him into the city—they rode a train just like the ones in this station. (The movie would flash back to the scene.)

Ben was three years old and riding on a train with his nanny when a lady gave birth. Ben's nanny was the closest thing to a doctor, so Ben had been by her side and had experienced an up-close view of this baby coming into the world. It was the most amazing thing that had ever happened to him, and he had never told a single soul about it.

He was never supposed to be on that train in the first place, and could never tell anyone it happened as long as he didn't want to get in trouble and get his nanny fired.

Ben told Anna that he could hardly get the words out to tell her this story, because it had been wedged securely in his heart for so many years. But it was his earliest and most beautiful memory, and one that would stick with him for the rest of his life.

He hadn't been looking at her, and by the time he finished telling the story, silent tears streamed down Anna's face. She knew Ben had just described the circumstances of her own birth. She knew in her heart that she was the baby in Ben's story.

He notices her crying, and they fumble over words and then share a moment where he instinctually kisses her.

It was a tender moment. The whole movie had been building to this, and their dialogue had me on the verge of crying and desperately feeling like I wanted them to beat the odds and be together forever.

Then suddenly, Anna was shaken from her trance when she hears an announcement that it was the last call for her train. She scrambles to pick up her bags and rushes off, saying goodbye to Ben and that it had been absolutely magical to meet the boy who was there when she came into the world.

She stares back at him through the window, feeling like it was a sign from God that everything was going to be all right. (There would be internal monologue at the end of the movie stating that.)

I set down the script with a sigh, feeling an odd mix of happy and sad. I wanted Ben and Anna to be together so badly, and I was sad when she rode away. But in my mind, there was still hope—if they had found each other twice, they could do it a third time.

I sat there, feeling all shaken up by the script.

I loved Anna, and I desperately wanted to play her. She was everything I wasn't. She came from nothing, and she had no help in life and no hope. I felt challenged to become her, and I instantly started sifting through my own feelings. I felt like I could play Anna and do it without being presumptuous. I wanted to try.

I could not stop thinking about it.

I picked up the script and read it in parts during the remainder of the night. I loved it, but there were unanswered questions that kept coming up in my mind.

It was late, and I was about to go to bed when I decided to compose an email to the writer.

Chapter 4

You should never ever compose an email late at night or when you're tired.

You should never compose one when you're emotional about something.

I was exhausted *and* emotional, and yet I still wrote to the author and sent it.

From: lmorgan11@vmail.com
To: wesleyquinn@quinnproductions.com
Re: Full Circle script

Hello Mr. Quinn,

My name is Lila Morgan, I am an actor, and I was given the Full Circle script by Mr. Frank Quinn. I read the script today, and I wanted to let you know how much I enjoyed it. What a great story! I didn't expect to enjoy it as much as I did. I just can't get over him being there at her birth. In my mind, they end up together even though the film doesn't show it. I am under the impression that I would be reading for the part of Anna. I was wondering when you were planning on filming and for how long. I am also curious about who's directing it and if you have cast any of the other roles. Thank you for your time and consideration,

Lila Morgan

I felt like I had done the right thing by sending it, but the following day, when I hadn't heard back from him, I began to doubt myself.

I felt like I should have contacted Frank Quinn and not the writer directly, but his contact information was right on the front of the script.

It was 4pm the following day when I finally saw a response in my email.

From: wesleyquinn@quinnproductions.com
To: lmorgan11@vmail.com
Re: Full Circle script

Hello, Ms. Morgan,

I will try to answer all of your questions. I wrote and will direct this movie. Ben will be played by Ryder Thorne. It is a small-budget film with a small production crew. Filming will take place here in Houston. I hope to start mid-March. I'm waiting on a permit, but I should have that and have all of my actors lined up by then. The plan is to have your part wrapped within a month. Some of the flashback scenes might happen after the scenes in the train station, but I need to have Anna and Ben's finished within a month for Ryder's sake.

Thanks, Wes

I began writing back instantly.

From: lmorgan11@vmail.com
To: wesleyquinn@quinnproductions.com
Re: Full Circle script

Hello Mr. Quinn,

Thank you so much for getting back to me. I just wanted to clarify that I am being considered for the role of Anna in this movie. I figured there would be a formal audition somewhere, and I wanted to let you know that I was interested in going to it and reading for this role.

Thank you, Lila

I heard back from him within a few minutes.

From: wesleyquinn@quinnproductions.com
To: lmorgan11@vmail.com
Re: Full Circle script

Hello,

I'm happy to hear you like the role and are interested. Please attach a video of yourself reading pages 78-80. It is Anna telling a story, so it's a monologue. I look forward to hearing from you.

Wes

My heart started pounding when I read his email. *Was I really doing this?* I hadn't even asked Frank Quinn if doing this movie meant I could no longer go to California afterward. I wondered if that was asking too much.

I decided to write Wesley back since he had been responding quickly to my emails.

From: lmorgan11@vmail.com
To: wesleyquinn@quinnproductions.com
Re: Full Circle script

Hello again Mr. Quinn,

Thank you so much. I will look at those pages and get an audition video to you by tomorrow afternoon.

Best, Lila

I wrote some other questions about whether or not he was related to Frank Quinn and if his first name had anything to do with the coffee shop in his office building. But then I deleted them and just sent the one-sentence email.

I would need to contact Frank Quinn to see how this audition would affect my General Hospital goals.

But in the meantime, I went to page seventy-eight to start memorizing that monologue.

It was Anna telling the story of the time her stepdad made her run up and steal a potted plant from someone else's porch to give it to her mom for Mother's Day. Anna's story was sad on so many levels, but I imagined her telling it with a good attitude.

I read it six or eight times, trying to feel Anna and hoping I would get somewhere in the ballpark of what Wesley envisioned. I didn't want to make her too dramatic or self-pitying.

For the remainder of the evening, I went over it. I read it a hundred times. I had it memorized, but I still made bullet point notes in case I lost my place or got distracted.

I slept on it.

I had to work from eight to two at the hospital, and during my shift, I sent an email to Frank Quinn telling him that I was auditioning for the role of Anna in the indie film but that I was still very much interested in going out west afterward if that was okay. I thanked him again for the opportunity.

I sent that email fairly early in the morning, and I still hadn't heard back from Frank at two when I left work.

I was focused on the script, anyway. I went over it in my head all day. I practiced several times when I got home that afternoon, and then I started filming my audition.

I did it in one take, and I didn't watch the results when I finished.

I texted it to my brother who was never afraid to be honest with me. I gave him a summary of the short film and asked him to watch the video for technical errors or glitches.

He texted me back with two words, "It's great," which was high praise coming from Beck.

I couldn't believe how badly I wanted this role. I felt challenged by it. I hated that the movie had a bittersweet ending, but I also loved that about it. I felt like Anna was better off as a person after that one serendipitous conversation with Ben.

The story stuck with me, and I took it as a personal challenge to make sure that Anna was played properly. I knew I was a beginner and it was probably egotistical for me to think I could play a lead role and be great my first time, but I knew in my heart that I could represent Anna, and I cared enough to make it the best possible performance.

I sent the audition to Wesley Quinn without watching it myself. It was late afternoon when I sent it, and I attached it in that same email thread from the day before.

I felt doubtful just after I sent it, and I went instantly to my sent folder and checked the email and the file to make sure it was all there. I went from hardly having the desire to do the audition to shaking in my boots as I waited to hear back from Wesley.

Chapter 5

It was an hour or so later when my phone rang. The call came from an unknown phone number with a Houston area code, and I picked it up on the first ring. I was alone in my apartment. I had been checking my email every ten minutes or so, but what came was a call.

"Hello?" I said.

"Is this Lila Morgan?" he asked.

"Yes."

"This is Wes Quinn."

"Wes, as in Wesley who wrote the screenplay?"

"Yes, but I go by Wes. Nobody ever calls me Wesley."

"Oh, I'm sorry. I thought since it was written on the script."

"My grandfather thinks there's already directors named Wes, Wes Anderson, Wes Craven… he said if I wanted to make a name for myself, it needed to be as Wesley. He never has liked the shortened version of my name. I wrote Wes on the screenplay, and he had his secretary change it before it got to you. That's why it took a while to respond to your first email. I forget to check that account."

"Wow," I said. I thought back to Frank Quinn saying he didn't fully trust the director. I assumed their relationship was strained. "Frank Quinn is your grandfather?"

"Yes. He might not admit that right now, but I'm his only grandson, so he doesn't have much of a choice."

"Why wouldn't he admit it?" I asked.

"He's mad at me because I spent half of my trust in what he thought was too short a time. He took the other half back."

"Did he really?" I asked. "I've never heard of that."

"I don't regret it. I traveled the world, I gave some of it away, and I have investments my grandfather knows nothing about. I still have some money tied up, but he thinks I lost it."

"Well, at least he's involved in your movie," I said.

"You're right, I'm thankful for that. He just doesn't like me very much. He and I are different. It was my mom who talked him into giving me some production assistance with this movie. Maybe I shouldn't tell you that. It's going to be great."

"Yeah, you could make it a big hit, and then he'll be happy he helped."

"Are you always so positive?" he asked.

"I try to be."

"Your audition was amazing."

"You liked it?" I asked, my heart suddenly pounding. "I wasn't sure what kind of delivery you imagined, so I just went with what I thought was—"

"It's great," he said. "I want you. I would love for you to play Anna. I think you'd be perfect."

"Oh my gosh, really?"

"Yes, but don't get too excited," he said.

"Why?"

"Money. You might still want to go to California at these rates. Ryder is doing my movie for free. We're friends, and he owes me. Unfortunately, with my money tied up in investments, all I can get access to for you is four-thousand dollars. It's about a thousand a week, which I know is terrible considering how much I'm going to need you. I'm going to ask you to have the script mostly memorized before we meet, and then I'll need access to you quite a bit during that month so that I can make sure I get good takes of all the scenes. I wanted to let you know because—"

"I'll do it," I said, cutting in. "I just got finished doing a play with a theater group. It was three months of work, and I did not get paid. I had to pay them to do it. Plus, I had to buy my own shoes and wig for the show."

"You might have to buy a few costume pieces with this as well. I don't know what I want Anna to wear. I'm having a friend of mine help me with costumes. That's not my forte. Her name is Gretchen. You'll be in touch with her once we get started, and she'll help you with costumes. I still have a lot of planning to do, but I would love to work with you, Lila."

"I just wanted to clarify that it's the first movie I've ever done," I said.

"Me too," he agreed with a little laugh.

"I really like the screenplay."

"Thank you."

"In my mind, they get together. Anna and Ben. Is there going to be a part two? Because in my heart, the two of them end up together."

"What? No," he said as if that idea never occurred to him. "It doesn't matter if they get together or not. They don't get together, but what matters is that she knows she's important—worthy. It was a coincidence only God could have orchestrated, so basically she found God in that moment."

"I know, and I feel bad for thinking about romance," I said. "They're just so good together."

"I'm sure you're not the only one. I bet some in the audience will take the kiss as meaning something, but it's just symbolic that she's loved—that she's alive for a reason."

"Wow, I guess that makes it a happy ending. I was kind of seeing it as bittersweet."

"No, it's definitely happy."

I smiled at his certainty, and I was glad he couldn't see me.

"This is off-topic, and I'm sorry if it seems nosy for me to ask, but are you the same Wes from Wesley's coffee?"

"I am. But it's not my business. It's my mother's. She named it after me years ago. I was only two years old when she started it."

"You must have a pretty cool mom," I said. "I love Wesley's."

"Me too. Thank you. She is a cool lady. She's the go-between with me and my grandfather—the buffer."

"Thank you for being so honest. My dad is the Chief of Surgery at Houston Methodist. He worked very hard to make your grandfather healthy again, and therefore your grandfather has agreed to get me an acting job. It's something I want to try, and I will do it on my own even if things don't work out with you or with General Hospital."

"General Hospital? *That's* what you want to do?"

"Why not?" I asked.

"Because it's cheesy," he said.

"No, it's not. And, even if it was, you shouldn't talk that way about your grandfather's..." I trailed off because I realized I was talking to my director and I needed to use respect. "I like cheesy stuff," I said diplomatically. Wes was laid back and easy to talk to, and I had gotten carried away.

"Should I take offense to that since you said you like my screenplay?" he asked.

I laughed. "Your movie isn't cheesy at all," I said. "It would probably be cheesy if you did what I said to do and have them run off together and get married and have babies."

He laughed. "If you feel that way, I'm sure other people do, too. Maybe someone will write fanfiction where Anna and Ben get a happily ever after."

"The more we talk about it, the more I'm starting to like it better how it is."

"Well, I'm glad because I'm not taking rewrites. I might be open to change if it's something I really like, but not this. I love the ending."

"I actually love the ending, too. I'm sorry I brought it up."

"Are you just saying that because I said I'm not asking for your opinion?"

"No, I actually do like the ending now. It is a happy ending."

"It is happy. Any more happiness would be too much."

"There's where we maybe don't agree, but I can see, artistically, what you're saying."

"So, you think you can't get too much happiness?" he asked.

"No. Of course not. Who would turn down happiness? I say pile it on."

He laughed at me. I liked him already, and I had high hopes that this movie would be a fun experience.

"Ryder is a friend of mine. He's got a busy schedule, but he's available for a few weeks during the end of March and beginning of April. Can you make that happen? Can you be prepared by then and ready to give a lot of your time during those weeks?

I'd like to get together with both of you soon, just to hear you read it and give you any notes. That way you can rehearse."

"I'd love that," I said. "I'd love any notes you have."

"Okay. Unfortunately, Ryder's in Peru and he won't be able to practice in person with you until we get together in March. I'll call Ryder and try to set up a time when we can all do a conference call or Zoom if you're comfortable with that."

"That sounds great," I said. "Thank you."

We talked for another minute, but quickly we hung up, leaving me in a dazed state. I could not believe I had officially taken a movie role. I loved Anna's character and I could not wait to get started.

***

It was just a few days later when I received a call from Ryder Thorne. He texted me first asking if I had time to take a quick phone call.

"Let's surprise Wes," was the first thing he said to me.

"What? What do you mean?"

"Let's FaceTime each other and practice the script together. Let's leave Wes out of it. I really love this script, and I feel like we can understand what he wants. I feel like you and I can work it out and surprise him. Would you be willing to try that? He's my boy, so I know he likes this type of thing."

"Yeah, I guess, if you're sure. I don't mind working with you, if you think you know what he wants."

"It's a good screenplay isn't it?"

"Yes, I really like it."

"I know his style, too. He's going to do a good job with the camera work and everything."

"I was excited about it before I knew any of that," I said. "I think the script is funny and raw and captivating."

"Me too. I read it last night and I was like duuuude… what's your name?"

"What, oh, my name? Lila. Lila Morgan."

"Where'd Wes find you? What kind of work have you done?"

"I've only done on-stage musicals, and only two of them. This is my first acting job but I'll do my best to be prepared and hold my own—not hold you back. I really like this character, and I'm going to try to keep up."

"I don't care what you do as long as we're done by April eighth. I'm going back to Spain on the ninth."

Chapter 6

Two months later
Mid-March

I now had Anna's role completely memorized. I had the script ingrained in my mind so firmly that I could almost say it backward and forward. My father had taught me how to be a determined student, and I knew how to practice something until I mastered it.

I practiced this screenplay relentlessly. My parents still supported me in some aspects of life, but they had quit paying my phone, groceries, and car insurance when I quit school. I worked to pay for those things, but every waking moment that I had off work was spent practicing my lines.

My family knew that I had been studying for a part in a movie, but none of them got the full scope of what was going on or how hard I was working.

I had gotten an email last week from Gretchen. It seemed as if she was doing a lot with the movie including acting as Wes's assistant. She introduced herself, saying she would be working with me for wardrobe, hair, and makeup. She attached about ten photographs to give me style inspiration and asked me to come camera-ready and dressed as close to the photos as possible, but that she would help adjust me as needed.

None of the correspondence was formal, but I was excited about it all the same.

Now the day was finally here.

I arrived on the set at noon even though I knew we wouldn't start filming until 3pm.

The flashback scenes would start next week and those would be held off-site at other locations. I was involved with a few of those, but not all of them. The majority of the movie was going to be shot in a train station.

That being said, the sun and its position was a part of this movie. It shone into the train station through windows that cast light across the floor and visually added to the shot.

It was gorgeous.

I loved the setting.

I had gone there the day before to scope it out.

The only problem with the sun-on-the-floor thing was that we only had a thirty-minute window every day to film this movie. As the movie progressed, we could start and go a little later, but for now, we were filming at 3pm sharp and we would be on a strict time schedule. We had plans to get together an hour early to prepare and rehearse for day one with Ryder.

I made my way up to the train station at noon so that I could work my wardrobe out with Gretchen and be prepared for rehearsal and filming. I hadn't met Wes yet, which was another reason I wanted to be there early.

There were two large white trailers in the parking lot of the train station. They were discreetly marked with the logo QTVP, which I knew stood for Quinn Television Productions.

At least his grandfather let him use some nice trailers, I thought as I approached the first, larger one. It had been locked the day before, but today, I knocked on the door, and Gretchen opened it. I knew it was her because she had on an apron with a name tag. She was a redhead—not natural, more of a cranberry-maroon color. But it looked great on her, and I smiled at the sight of her. Her eyes widened as she took in my appearance.

"Oh my gosh, you look just like Anna! You look just like the photos I sent you!"

She reached out and pulled me into the trailer. It was full of props and costumes—most of the things that would be used for the flashback sequences, but I couldn't process that at the time. It was all just foreign clutter to me, and all of it felt overwhelming and exciting.

"I saw your audition, and your hair was darker. Did you have your hair highlighted?"

"Oh, yes, I did," I said, grabbing at my hair, which I was wearing down and styled over my shoulders.

I tried to make it look like the inspiration Gretchen had sent me because she said Wes helped her pick it out and it was what he wanted.

"Did you do that for the movie?" she asked.

"Y-yes," I said, almost feeling like I was walking into a trap.

"Aw, Wes, she had her hair lightened for the movie, isn't that so sweet? Come see her. She's amazing—just like the photos. This jacket, girl! It's exactly the one in the picture. Was this *your* jacket? Did you own this?"

I had gone to great lengths to obtain this jacket. I had to go through a friend of a friend. It was vintage and very hard to come by.

"I bought it for the movie," I said simply.

"Wes, she had her hair highlighted and bought a jacket. She looks just like the photographs I sent her!"

Gretchen had her head turned and projected her voice to the other side of the trailer.

Then from behind a wall, came Wes.

My heart dropped when I realized who it was.

I couldn't breathe.

I should have guessed it. I should have put the pieces together. The guy from the coffee shop was staring back at me. I froze and my mind raced. He had already seen me. He watched my audition and he knew what I looked like. He had seen me and he didn't mention our encounter in the coffee shop. I stared at him. I thought maybe I shouldn't bring it up either.

"Whoa, Anna. You're Anna! Thank you, Lila. It's really great. You captured her. Now, do you think you can do exactly this for the next three weeks? Don't change a thing."

"I can't promise my hair won't grow, but I'll do my best."

He stared at me, looking me over and nodding. "Wow, thank you. The costume is perfect, don't you think?" He looked at Gretchen who had already moved on to hot-gluing something at a workstation.

"That's what I was telling you. Isn't she wonderful? She's perfect."

Wes took a seat in a nearby director's chair. He was a sight to behold. He had been so slumped over that day in the coffee shop that I had no concept of his stature. My brother was six-foot tall, and this guy was at least that tall. He was thick and broad-chested without looking beefy. His form was impeccable. I got lost staring at him… wondering what his story was. Now that he was sitting up, I could see his muscles through his shirt. He looked like he was no stranger to a gym. He was way too big for this trailer. He nudged his chin at me and smiled. My breath grew heavier and I was doing nothing but standing there.

"Did you and Ryder get it worked out?" he asked.

"What did you say?"

"Did you have time to go over some lines with Ryder?"

"Oh yeah, we've talked a few times. We worked it out. He said he told you. He said he wanted to surprise you."

"Yeah, that's what he told me, too. How's it coming together?"

"I think it's good, but I guess you'll tell me what you think in a little while," I said.

"Ryder will be here an hour before we're ready to shoot," he said. "But I can walk over to the station with you in a minute. I'm still debating about which side of the bench I'm going to have you sit."

"I imagined I'd be sitting where Ryder was on my right," I said.

"Why?" he asked.

I smiled and shrugged. "The script didn't specify, and I just imagined it that way."

"Have you talked to Ryder about it?"

"No, why?"

"He might have a preference, I'm not sure. How flexible are you if he does?"

"I really don't care where I sit, honestly."

"Okay, well, I'll take a look at the shot with you in it, and we'll make the call. I'll make sure you feel comfortable. I bet Ryder won't care. I'm going to get out of here for now. Gretchen will help make sure you're camera ready. You might want to take pictures of what she looks like, Gretchen, so we can be consistent."

"I will, thanks for reminding me," she said, nodding as she looked at me.

"I'm going outside," Wes said. "I'll meet you out here in a few minutes, Lila, and we can check out the set."

I nodded at him and let him walk out. I didn't remind him that we had seen each other before.

"Wes is the best," Gretchen said, whispering to me when he closed the door. "He's crazy good at everything he does. I've had a crush on him since I can remember." She rolled her eyes at herself, smiling. "I follow him around like a puppy dog, going along with all his crazy ideas. And the thing is, they usually turn out amazing. Everything he does turns to gold. He's wonderful. Do you know he's traveled the world? He, himself, actually saw somebody have a baby right in front of him in India. That's what made him think of this storyline."

She paused and looked at me, and I just smiled at her because I wasn't sure what else to do.

"It's a really good storyline," I said. "That's what made me want to do the movie. I didn't realize he saw a live birth, though."

"Do you know Wes?" she asked.

"I don't. I met him just now for the first time. His grandfather knows my father, and I was going to try a thing on General Hospital, but then I read this script, and I really loved it."

"Well, Wes deserves the best. I think we should all do what we can to make it as good as it can be."

She leaned in with an intense expression, whispering even more quietly than she had been before. "His grandparents gave him two million dollars and they took a million of it back."

I made a face like that must've hurt.

"Yeah. Wes gave a few hundred thousand to a friend who is working with renewable resources. They're making developments with wind energy and electric cars, and Wes is really forward thinking and amazing, so he invested. His family thinks he got scammed. They're really mean to Wes. Frank thinks that Wes is too soft because he wants to travel and he doesn't care about money. He took away a million dollars. Can you imagine if someone gave you a million and then took it away?"

"No, I can't," I said. "But at least we still get to use the trailer and stuff."

I felt like a total square for saying that, but I didn't want to get caught talking bad about Mr. Quinn. It was his trailer, after all. As far as I was concerned, he was the one giving me this opportunity.

Gretchen scoffed when I said that. "This trailer is nothing. Franklin Quinn threw him some scraps. You should see all the trailers and equipment they have at the studio. He's got whole production teams, and he gives Wes access to *two trailers* and *two people*—a PA and a cameraman?" She rolled her eyes and sighed as if thinking about it upset her, then went back to whatever she was doing with the hot glue gun.

But I didn't feel so jaded. If I wanted to make a movie and my grandfather gave me a budget (no matter how small) with two trailers and two employees, I would think that was pretty generous. I didn't say as much to Gretchen, though, I just kept my mouth shut.

She scowled at her work.

"I'm sure it helps that a lot of the movie takes place on a bench," I said, making more positive conversation.

"That makes it easy. Yeah, but we have ten flashback scenes to film. It's fine, though. Wes will make it work. We'll figure out a way to turn a mountain into a molehill."

I stared at Gretchen after she said it. She was completely serious and believed she had used the phrase correctly, so I just didn't say anything. I thought about what she said, and I had to fight the urge to laugh, but I distracted myself, looking around the trailer.

"Ouch," she said, fanning her hand through the air as if to cool it.

"Did you need to put a mic on me or take pictures?" I asked.

She regarded me from head to toe, looking me over. "Not yet. It's a little early. I had you get here early because I thought I would need to touch you up, but you look great. You did a great job at being camera ready—made up, but also tired and ragged."

"Thanks," I said smiling stiffly at the odd compliment.

I could tell she distanced herself from me slightly when I didn't jump onboard with assuming the worst about Frank Quinn, but I had never been much of a gossiper.

"It's really cool that Wes is doing this, though, even if his budget isn't the best. It's a great story."

"Uh-hm. Hey, you can go check in with Wes since he wanted to take you inside the station."

"Yeah, yeah, that's fine. I was just hanging out since I thought you needed me. But if you don't need to do that now, then I'll go out here." I made my way to the door. "Okay, great, thank you. Well, I'll see you in a little bit, I guess."

"Yep, just go out there and find Wes."

I smiled at her, but I left the trailer feeling a little confused. She was really happy to see me when I first got there, but toward the end of our conversation, her demeanor had changed somewhat. I figured that maybe she was just like that as a person. I told myself to smile and do what they told me in an effort to try to get along with everyone. I was nervous in general. It was my first day on set and I had never met Ryder or Wes.

Wes was intimidating.

He was standing right next to the door when I opened it, and he looked up at me and reached out to help me down. I held his hand, and my heart turned to hot liquid when we touched. My insides were on fire. All this from a man reaching out to help me down the steps.

I had barely ever seen Wes, and I had only talked to him about the movie, but touching his hand made my knees weak. He was just that good-looking. He was the type of good looking where it was distracting. His dark eyes seemed to pierce through me. I was aware of his masculinity and attracted to him in a way I rarely, if ever, experienced with men. It caused physical reactions in me.

I held his hand just long enough to step off of the trailer—and take one step onto the pavement. Then I promptly let it go. I peered up at him and smiled, doing my best to seem unaffected and calm. "I'm excited to play Anna," I said.

Chapter 7

Wes Quinn
Three weeks later

Today was the final day of shooting with Ryder and Lila, and Wes was not looking forward to it at all.

It was the dreaded kiss.

They had to film the kissing scene, and Wes had put it off until the very last day. They had to get it done today because Ryder was leaving for Spain in the morning.

Wes should've never waited this long to make the scene happen, but he couldn't bear to let the two of them kiss each other. He didn't know he would develop these feelings when he first hired Lila, but he grew to like her during the last few weeks, and now he could not think about watching her mouth touch Ryder's.

He was already annoyed by how much chemistry they had while they were acting. And to think—he was pumped about their chemistry at first. As a director, he loved seeing how natural his two main characters were together and how well they got along. But that didn't last long. Soon, their on-screen connection started to annoy Wes.

Of course, he never let on to either of them that he was jealous.

No one knew.

Lila had no idea that he wanted her.

They thought he was putting off the kissing scene for other, scheduling reasons—Wes had led them to believe that. But today was the day. They could put it off no longer. It was 3:30pm, and they were scheduled to start shooting now.

Wes was never ever late, but he did not want to do this scene and it was impossible to make himself walk over to the train station and get started.

"I'll be right there!" he yelled to the group of people standing around the dreaded bench.

Wes made his way to the bathroom, feeling like he might be sick. He went to the sink and ran cold water, using it to splash onto his face.

He looked in the mirror.

He had done this to himself.

He put Lila in a position where he had to sit there and watch her kiss someone else. Wes had orchestrated the whole thing. He tried to remind himself of that. But back then, he had no idea he would feel this way about Lila. He had no idea he would fall for her. His heart raced, and he felt like wanted to punch Ryder Thorne in the face.

He held onto the sides of the sink and stared into his own dark eyes, begging himself to see this for what it was—a movie—his movie. He needed to think of the movie. He took a deep breath and tried on a fake smile before turning and walking out.

The whole thing passed in a blur. Wes knew all the things he should do as a director to make the scene happen. He put his feelings on the back burner and watched the two of them say their lines and then kiss each other.

"Cut! Okay, Ryder… that's…"
Wes came up to them, heart pounding.
"When you go in, Ryder. You need to put your hands here and here." Wes took Lila's hand in one hand and put his other hand on her back, pulling her into his embrace. "Make it look like you're trying to stop yourself but you just can't understand your own feelings."

Wes glanced at Lila when he said that and he lost his train of thought. *What was he even saying?* He was the one who couldn't understand his own feelings. He felt a jolt of electricity and he dropped her hand, stepping back and letting Ryder get back into position. His muscles felt weak after the wave of adrenaline. He went through the rest of the scene on autopilot.

He was livid at Ryder for kissing Lila, and yet he had to sit there and watch it five more times until they got it blasted right. And then, when Ryder finally did a good job, it made Wes want to punch him all the more.

They were there for forty-five minutes, working intently while the sun was in the right position on the floor of the train station.

It was by far the hardest day for Wes, but from a theatrical standpoint, it went well. The acting was good, and he was sure they got the shot. They had already filmed the scene where she got on the train, but they went ahead and did it again since everything was going well and it was Ryder's last day.

This gave Wes time to cool off. He got to watch Anna get on the train without any kind of romantic happily ever after.

They had already filmed the one where she actually rode away, so all they did this time was let the door close before the engineer re-opened it.

Wes had time to catch his breath after the kissing scene, but he was still fighting against jealous feelings that no one else knew anything about. Gretchen was doing nothing to help the situation. She kept making remarks about how she wished Ryder and Lila would get together in real life.

Wes kept it all bottled up inside. He smiled and pretended to be normal. He directed the scene, and now it was over. It was finally over. All of the shooting with Ryder and Lila was complete.

"It's a wrap," he said, smiling. "At least with you, Ryder. I've got one more scene at the high school with you, Lila."

"That's crazy that I'm done, bro," Ryder said reaching out to hug Wes. "This movie's gonna be so good, dawg, I'm telling you. I can't wait to see it."

"Thanks for being here and doing this, Ryder," Wes said. "I really appreciate it."

Ryder casually reached out and hugged Lila. "It was absolutely my pleasure," Ryder said. "I loved every second of it." He was hugging Lila when he said it, and Wes felt like he wanted to tackle him to the ground like a mad linebacker on steroids.

"Okay, well, that's awesome. I know you have to be going, so let me let you let me go… I mean, let me let you go. Lila, if I can see you in the trailer, please. We need to go over a few things for that high school scene." Wes patted Ryder on the shoulder again so it didn't seem awkward. "Thanks again, Ryder. I'm stoked about the footage we got and can't wait to start editing. Have fun in Spain."

Gretchen went to work helping Ryder, and Lila followed Wes into the trailer while the few others disbursed and began putting things away.

"I can't believe we're done in the train station," Lila said to Wes as they walked.

He glanced at her before opening the door for her. "I know. I can't believe it either. This day came much sooner than I expected."

She nodded. "No kidding. I'm going to really miss making this movie."

They were outside now, and Wes walked beside Lila as they headed toward the trailer. "What are you going to miss about it?" he asked. "Working with Ryder?"

"No, just the whole thing. I'll miss everything. I'll miss Gretchen fussing over every piece of my hair being the same. And most of all, I'll miss kissing Ryder." Wes's head whipped around and he stared at Lila with wide eyes that made her laugh. "I'm just messing with you," she said. "That was the most awkward scene ever. I am so thankful you saved it for the last day. I've never, in my life, done anything like that before."

The two of them had talked about scenes openly during the last few weeks. They had grown close and had lots of lengthy conversations. But things were different today. He had to watch her get kissed and he realized he didn't like it. He didn't like it at all. He couldn't believe she was joking around about it.

"It was great. You guys did a great job," he said, trying to say the things he would normally say. He held open the trailer door and gestured for Lila to go inside. "I saw you in my mom's coffee shop," Wes added.

She stared at him like she was stunned to hear him say that.

"I heard you say you were going to see my grandfather, and I called him and told him I wanted you to be in my movie. I don't know if you remember me, but I stared at you for a long time that day."

She couldn't believe it. They had been working together all this time, and he was just now mentioning the coffee shop.

"I knew you'd be perfect for the role. I was stunned when I heard you say you were an actress and that you were going upstairs to see my grandfather."

"You heard me talking? You had on earbuds."

"You were two feet away and you weren't being quiet."

"I had no idea you heard me," she said, not knowing what else to say. "I knew I saw you that day, but I didn't know you called your grandfather. I thought it was a coincidence. I thought you didn't even remember seeing me in the coffee shop. We've been working together for a month. Why didn't you bring it up before today? You could have said it the first night I emailed you."

"It didn't matter then. When I hired you, I just knew I wanted you as an actress. I thought you would look good with Ryder."

"Do you not think that now?"

"No. I don't think that now," he said. He was letting his emotions get the best of him. He should not be talking to her like this. He needed to keep it professional. He had no problem doing that during the last three weeks, and he had no idea why today was so different.

That last take was amazing.

Lila looked like she really enjoyed it.

Wes's temper flared at the thought. "Just take your mic off and switch it off," he said, feeling frustrated and needing some task to concentrate on. "We still have to film that scene at the high school," he added.

"I know. I was waiting to hear from Gretchen about when we were going to do it," she replied. "She was telling me we have to schedule it on a Friday so our extras will be there."

"Yeah, it's this Friday," he said tossing his binder onto his desk.

"Are you okay?" Lila asked.

"Am I okay? Yeah, why?"

"I don't know, you look like you're upset."

"No, I'm just... I have a lot on my mind. I need to make some notes about things I saw during that session, and I've got a lot of other things on my mind."

She shrugged. "I'm sure it's hard to see Ryder go."

"Why would that be hard?" he asked, scowling.

"I don't know. You had told me about loving to travel, and I thought you might be looking forward to when you can do it again. I thought maybe it was bittersweet with him leaving for Spain."

"No. It's not bittersweet," Wes said. "I am fine with Ryder leaving. I'm glad he did the movie, but I'm fine with him leaving."

"What else is on your mind besides filming the next scene?" she asked. "You kind of seem like you're mad. I feel like I've done something wrong. If it wasn't good today, we can just go out there and shoot it again. Ryder was saying that he had some time before he needs to pack and—"

She cut off her sentence when Wes invaded her space. He stepped in front of her with his eyes closed and his head bowed like he was hoping she would embrace him. It was an out-of-character thing for Wes to do. Lila cautiously wrapped her arms around him.

She fished her hands between his arms and his body and held him around his middle, hugging him securely.

"Whatcha doin' Wes?" she asked after they were there for a few seconds.

The two of them were friends by now, but he had been dreading this day. He breathed, straightening and looking down at her. She pulled back and let go of him a little bit, but she still kept one hand on Wes.

"When I hired you, I was fine with you playing Anna. And then I started to realize that I might hate certain aspects of it. You and I keep things professional, and I don't want to say anything to make you uncomfortable, but that was not my favorite scene to film just now."

She smiled a little just before she reached up and kissed him on the cheek. She placed a sweet kiss on Wes's face, and he touched her waist, pulling her in. He felt like he might never let her go again. He might actually die if he couldn't make Lila Morgan his own.

He swallowed hard the instant her lips hit his skin, and just like that it was over, and he was thrust into reality. The trailer door was thrust open, light streaming into it. Wes was in a daze, but Lila didn't skip a beat. She was already two steps away from him by the time Gretchen appeared in the doorway.

Chapter 8

Lila Morgan

Oh, my goodness. What had just happened?

I had hugged Wes and then kissed his cheek, and I had meant both of them in a more-than-friends way. Wes was acting differently toward me, and I could not stop myself from responding to him.

He was in the middle of telling me that he liked me, and I had leaned in and kissed his cheek. It was slow and soft, and we might have moved forward to kissing on the mouth had we not been interrupted.

I had to stifle the urge to laugh nervously when Gretchen walked in. She came in talking as if nothing had happened. "He said he's going to cut his hair when he gets home," she said, talking about Ryder. "Am I interrupting something?" she added, looking at us.

"No," I said.

"Yes," Wes replied at the same time.

"We were talking about Friday," I said. "Are we filming at the school this Friday?"

"Yes, we are." She glanced at me. "I'll get more information to you soon about your costume and makeup. You'll need to be younger, so use a beauty treatment or whatever you have at home. Also, I might want you to cut bangs—or we can clip some in. See if you can find a clip-in at the beauty supply store."

I nodded, taking it all in.

"We've got a scene scheduled at the park with young Ben and about ten other kids tomorrow," she added, looking at Wes. "We've got our hands full all day."

"I need to get with Lila about some things I want to see in the school scene," Wes said. He looked at me. "Do you have time to grab a bite to eat tonight? Maybe around eight?"

I was terrified in this moment.

Wes had never done anything like this. He had never asked me out after hours. We ate meals together as a crew and spent a lot of time together on set. I had gotten to know him during the last few weeks, but he had never mentioned doing anything off-set, especially just the two of us.

I was also stunned because Gretchen was standing right there, and she had made her crush on Wes very, very clear—crystal clear. I had no confusion about her feelings for Wes. She announced them to me on a regular basis.

"Sure, yeah," I said. "I'd love to have your insights about that scene."

"I'll text you in a couple of hours, and we can figure out a place."

I did my best to seem nonchalant and casual as I gathered my things from the trailer. It only took a few seconds, and I was all finished—leaving the train station for what would probably be the last time. I hesitated at the door and wanted to make some kind of speech about how much I enjoyed making the movie with them, but I knew we weren't finished quite yet and that I would probably see Wes tonight.

Instead, I simply told the two of them goodbye and walked out.

***

It was a while later when I got a call from Wes. I was at my parents' house, and I picked up my phone on the first ring.

"Hello?" I said, turning my back to my family and walking away to get some privacy.

"Hey, where are you?" Wes asked.

"I'm at my mom's. She cooked tonight, so we were all over here."

"Oh, did you already eat?"

"No, I didn't yet. I didn't know if I would hear from you."

"You did hear from me," he said, and I smiled even though he couldn't see me.

"Did you want to meet somewhere?" I asked.

"Yes, I was hoping to. For dinner. Are you up for it?"

"Yeah, I am. I thought that's why you were calling."

"What about some tacos?"

"Yes, please," I said.

"I know a place that's between us. I can be there in one hour. I'll text you the address," he said.

"Sounds great. I can be there in an hour, too."

I was wholeheartedly smitten with Wes. I couldn't help it. Gretchen found his charms irresistible, and I was the same way. I told my parents and brother about my dinner plans and went to my apartment to get dressed.

I rushed and went out of my way to make myself look nice for him. I had to be plain-looking when I was playing Anna, and I curled my hair and wore clothes that Anna would never wear. I put on jeans and a light linen blouse since the weather was now getting warmer. I curled my hair and my eyelashes and I put on glittery lip gloss. I also wore scented lotion in addition to my perfume. I scrambled and tried hard to make myself presentable for him.

I had a crush on Wes Quinn since the moment I laid eyes on him in the coffee shop. I had worked with him for weeks and gotten to know him, and we had kept things professional, but I liked him so much.

And he looked at me differently today. Something had shifted with Wes, and I couldn't let that go unnoticed. I put a lot of effort into getting dressed for dinner and making sure everything was in the right place. Wes texted me the address of a Mexican restaurant, and I met him there.

I was ten minutes early, and I walked inside to find that he was already waiting for me when I arrived. Our eyes met as he stood up.

He had changed. Not just his clothing, but the way he was looking at me had changed. He was wearing nice, fitted clothes—jeans and a solid t-shirt. It was a dark plum color. My heart was going haywire. This all felt like a date.

"Hey," I said, crossing to him.

"Hey," Wes said, leaning in for the hug.

We embraced, and he pulled back with a smile.

"You look pretty," he said quietly to me. But someone else was in the room, and she was aware of us. The hostess had seen me come in, and she stood there and smiled at us. "There's just two of us," Wes said to her. And we took off walking, following her into the restaurant, which was mostly full.

She led us to a booth and we thanked her.

We barely had time to take a breath. We had just looked at each other when our server came by. It was another young woman who introduced herself, gave us water and chips, and took our drink order. "I've never been here before," I said, looking around as she walked away. My eyes quickly found Wes, and I smiled when I realized he was staring back at me. "Have you been here before?" I asked.

He nodded. "Lots of times."

"You can just order for me then," I said.

"I will," he agreed, accepting the challenge.

I handed him my menu, and he took it, looking surprised. "Really?"

"Yeah," I said.

"Is there anything you don't eat?"

"No," I said.

"How hungry are you?"

"Hungry enough for a meal?" I said uncertainly, hoping that explained enough to him.

He grinned at me. "Okay, I'll order for you."

"I'm still hung up on the fact that you called your grandfather that day. I can't believe you've known this whole time, and you haven't told me about it."

"I figured you knew," he said. "A lot of people know I'm Wes when I'm hanging out in that coffee shop. At first, I thought that was why you were staring at me."

"No."

I didn't even know what else I wanted to say. I was too caught up in the fact that he was sitting across from me at a restaurant.

"I can't believe I only have one scene left to film," I said. "I think the movie's going to be really good. I'm excited about being a part of it."

"Yeah, I'm excited about it, too. Thank you. Thank you for doing your best every day. You're a hard worker, and you're really good."

"Thank you," I said. "I'm just trying to do the script justice. It's a tall order."

"For a short girl," he said.

"Heyyyy, five-five is average."

"In Houston, maybe. I don't know about Hollywood."

I scrunched up my face at him. "You're just trying to get me to stay."

"I am trying. That's exactly what I'm doing. But I can't do that. You'll go, and you'll do great. The next director is going to love working with you just like I did."

"This sounds like a goodbye speech and I officially hate it," I said. "I left the trailer earlier today thinking about how it was the last time I would be at the train station, and I felt so sad about it. I really enjoyed this project."

"How long are you planning on being in California?" he asked.

"I'm leaving for Arkansas next week—going to my family's lake house. I'll be there for a few weeks, and then I'm coming home briefly before heading out west. I'm planning on being there for six months. I'll come back at Christmas. I'll either start back in medical school, or I'll keep pursuing acting. I'm giving myself six months to figure it out."

"What if you get a big role out there and you can't come back for Christmas?" he asked.

I smiled at him. "That's the dream, I guess, right? That's the goal, isn't it?"

"Yeah, I guess. So, you want to end up in Hollywood?"

I sighed. "I don't know what I want. I want to act—to try acting. I knew that. I've loved doing theater, and now a movie, and next I'm going to try a little TV. I have absolutely loved all of it, and even as an extra, I think TV will be a fun experience."

"What do your parents think about all this?"

"They're freaking out a little. They're both really strict."

"You said your dad's a surgeon and your mom was Miss Texas. You don't get to be those things without a certain level of discipline."

I bit down on a chip at the moment he said that, and I smiled and nodded, agreeing with him.

"They're both really strict in their work ethic, but it's not just that. They are big-time involved in the church. They are always doing church-related stuff. I'm spending three weeks at my uncle's house in Arkansas, and during the first week, I'll be with a group of women from the church."

"What about the other two?" he asked.

"I'll be with my brother and probably some family."

"The first one is with a bunch of women?"

I nodded. "They're all from my mom's church. It's a women's retreat."

"Oh, and you have to go for that?" he asked, smiling curiously at me.

"I want to," I said, grinning back at him. "Totally of my own free will. It's fun. Half of those women are people I knew growing up. They're comfortable and funny."

"What kind of stuff do y'all do?" he asked.

"Oh, you know, Bible study, Bible trivia, Bible memorization, prayer time." I smiled at him in such a way that he knew I was joking. "We go tubing and stuff on the lake. It's a gorgeous lake, and my uncle has nice boats. It's still cold that time of year, but we go on the water. They're just a bunch of goofballs. They'll stay for five or six days, and then it's just me and my brother for a couple of days until my family starts rolling in for the summer. Then I'm taking off for California."

"You enjoy hanging out with church people?" He asked the question as if he was sizing me up.

"Yeah. Is that a bad thing?"

"With you, Lila, I think nothing's bad. How many of you are going?"

"There's me and my mom, and eight or ten other women."

"Is the house big enough for all of you?"

"Oh, yeah, it's gigantic. I don't think anyone else in my family is going to be out there during that week. They usually start rolling in during the middle of May, but there's a ton of room. I'll bet thirty people could sleep there—especially with couches and air mattresses."

"That'll be fun," he said.

I stared at his mouth as it moved. I was captivated.

"I have a few more weeks of shooting before I start editing."

"And how long will that take you?" I asked.

"I set the release date for mid-January. I'm hoping I'll be done with it before Thanksgiving."

"Maybe you'll finish with your movie and I'll come back to visit for Christmas, and we can run into each other. You know, see each other for Christmas."

I was breathless with nerves and anticipation as I made that suggestion. Wes was my ideal man, full of talent and wisdom in a package that looked tough and reckless. And there he was, sitting across from me staring at me like he was interested in me. I closed my mouth, reaching out and grabbing the glass so that I could take a sip of water and distract myself.

Chapter 9

"I'd really like to run into you at Christmas, Lila," Wes said. "I hope things work out for you in California, but I'd also love for you to come home for Christmas. By the way, what did you do last night?" he added.

"What?"

"I heard you mention something to Aiden earlier about nursing classes."

"Oh, that. I'm taking a nursing class—not officially, but I'm going to nursing class with a friend of mine—as many of them as I can make. They're letting me observe. I'm taking notes since I might be cast as a nurse."

He shook his head and grinned a little at me like he just couldn't figure me out.

"I'm just being prepared," I said. "Even if I'm in the background as a nurse, I'll look more natural if I know a few things real nurses know."

"You're already studying for a roll you don't have yet?"

"Yes. Well, it is General Hospital. I can't go wrong watching a few nurses. I won't be nervous if I'm prepared."

"You're full of goodness," he said.

"What?"

"You are. Not just the church stuff, but also how you work for things. I feel like you're just good. Like goodness is what comes out of you. Are you just excellent at everything you do?"

"Are you asking if I'm a goody-two-shoes right now?" I asked, biting down on a full-size chip with salsa. "Because I have been called that," I said, after I chewed.

"No, I'm not asking that. I know we have a working relationship right now, Lila, and I know we'll both be busy for the next little while, doing our own things. But I was thinking maybe at Christmas, when you got back… since we wouldn't be working together. If you come back to Texas, I was wondering if you might want to—"

"Yes," I said.

He grinned at me and looked me over patiently. "I didn't ask anything yet."

"Oh, what were you going to ask?"

"What did you think I was going to ask?"

"You tell me what you were going to ask, and I'll tell you if that's what I thought."

"What did you agree to?" he asked.

"I know what I was going to agree to, but I want to hear you say it, just to make sure."

"I was going to ask if you would ever want to work with me again. You know, if I made another movie."

"Yeah, yep, and that's what I was agreeing to," I said. "I figured you were going to ask about a movie, so that's what I was talking about."

"Really? Is it?" he asked.

"Yes."

Both of us were quiet.

We each took another bite of chips.

"Because I wasn't really going to ask about a movie," he said. "I was lying."

My goodness.

We were flirting, and my insides were on fire because of it. I tried my best to keep my face neutral even though I wanted to grin from ear to ear.

"What *were* you talking about?" I asked.

"I was trying to ask you out."

I felt blood rush to my face, but I smiled and tried to keep it cool.

"I would've probably agreed to that, too," I said. "But I thought that was what we were doing here."

"This is not a date," he said. "This is strictly business. You'd know if it was a date."

"All right, then, never mind," I said, looking slightly offended.

"I want to go on a date with you, but I don't want you to think I thought that's what this is."

"Well, just know that I'm open to it happening on my end." I shrugged like I was casual and nonchalant.

"I'm open to it happening on my end," he said. "But your dad would probably be mad since I'm technically not in the best graces with my grandfather. Who knows what he's heard about me."

I made a confused face.

"What?" he asked.

"Me dating you has nothing to do with my dad."

"Just to be clear, Lila, I want to take you out. I want to take you out multiple times." He took a deep breath and sat up straight. "I hope this isn't too much information or anything, but I felt like I wanted to crack Ryder's skull open today. I know I wrote the scene and hired you guys to perform it, so I get it that it's insane of me to admit, but I got myself into a little bit of a bind today because I didn't know I would have a problem with watching you guys do that."

"And you did?" I asked.

"Yes, I did."

"Well, it was weird for me, too. But for the sake of the scene, and to make it believable, I had to pretend that I liked kissing Ryder."

"You don't have to say it. You don't have to say his name."

I tilted my head and squinted at Wes. "I was happy when you asked me to meet you here tonight, Wes. It might get me killed, and I was still happy about it."

"What do you mean, it might get you killed?"

"Gretchen," I said.

He let out a little sound that was similar to a laugh.

"I'm serious," I said. "She's in love with you, and she's vicious about it."

Wes shrugged. "Just be vicious back," he said.

I breathed a laugh.

"I'm only here with one person, aren't I?"

"I thought you said this was strictly business," I said.

"I might've lied about that."

"I can't keep up," I said. "What's the truth and what's a lie?"

"I like you, Lila," he said. "Let me make it simple. I like you so much. I know I'm not supposed to like you because I'm your director, but I would love it if this was a date."

"I have church friends," I said.

He shrugged, staring at me with a confused expression. "That, unbelievably, makes me like you more. I love that you're a good girl."

"Never been kissed before today," I said.

"Yeah right," he said, smiling as he chewed.

"I haven't."

He let out a little laugh. "You're joking," he said.

I shook my head, wearing a serious expression. I wasn't joking.

"Why are you shaking your head? You've been kissed before," he said, as if he was certain.

"No, I haven't. Y-you know if you don't count today," I added shrugging. "First Ryder, and then you—sort of—on the cheek."

My voice was tentative, and Wes's expression became gravely serious. He stared at me intensely as he sat up and got to the edge of his seat. "Look at me, Lila. Don't mess around. I love joking around, but be serious for a second, please. Have you ever kissed a guy before today?"

"No, I haven't, Wes." "I honestly haven't. They were thinking about having me kiss Seaweed during Hairspray, but we just faked it."

He cleared his throat. "Ryder Thorne was the first guy you've ever kissed?"

Wes choked out the words seriously, and I nodded. He cleared his throat again and stood up. I could see the muscle in his jaw twitch as he looked away dramatically.

"How can… hold on a minute, I'll be right back."

I watched as Wes walked away, toward the front of the restaurant while I was left there with the chips and salsa. I took a drink of water. Wes was only gone for a minute, and my heart raced as I watched him cross the restaurant and sit down again. His masculine body was so wound up that I could see tension in his demeanor. I could not help but smile.

Wes rubbed his jaw as if looking for the right words, but before he could get anything out, our server appeared out of nowhere, asking if we were ready to order. "Two quesadillas. One steak and one chicken. Just, however it normally comes is fine."

"Okay, one fajita steak quesadilla and one fajita chicken quesadilla… is that going to be all? Would you like any appetizers—cheese or guacamole, to come out first?"

"Sure," he said without looking at her. He had not taken his eyes off of me.

"Which one would you like?" she asked.

"All of them. Whatever is fine. Just anything you mentioned is fine."

"What appetizer would you like?"

"The first one listed on the menu," he said.

"The… mini tacos?" she asked hesitantly.

"Sure."

She got the picture that Wes was preoccupied, and she thanked us before taking our menus and leaving.

Wes took a deep breath. "Okay, Lila. Let me just be straightforward. Please tell me you've kissed someone before today," he said.

"I cannot tell you that," I said. "Unless you want me to lie."

"Did you and Ryder not practice? I thought you practiced."

"We practiced lines. We didn't practice the kiss. Why do you think it took us so many takes?"

He made a face like he was in pain. "Why didn't you tell me this before, Lila?"

"Would it have changed anything?" I asked.

"Yes, I would not have let you kiss him."

"You *had* to let me kiss him. That was the whole movie. The whole movie boils down to that kiss."

"No, it doesn't. I almost took it out today, anyway. I should have. I can't believe you let me do that. How have you gone through life and not let that happen with anyone?"

He was completely serious, and I bit my lip to hold in a nervous smile. "I told you, my parents were strict. They knew everything I did. And then, once I came to be of age, I just haven't found anyone who gave me the urge."

"I thought you said you had boyfriends," he said, remembering a conversation we had on set. "I have had boyfriends, but I haven't done that with any of them."

"Because you're that strict?" he asked. "Are you not allowed to kiss a guy with your church or something?"

"No," I said, laughing. "I dated people and had opportunities in high school and college, but I just didn't want to. I never wanted to."

"And you wanted to let it happen meaninglessly with Ryder Thorne?" he asked, looking horrified.

I laughed a little at his facial expression. "I didn't want to, necessarily, but it was a job. I was acting. It was what Anna would do, and I needed to do it. I don't have a moral code against kissing a guy, I just never wanted to. I wanted to today simply because I wanted to get the job done."

"And you're okay kissing a guy even when you don't have feelings about it?"

"Am I in trouble right now? Is that why you invited me here?"

"No. When I invited you here I had no idea you had *never kissed anyone*."

He whispered intensely and I blinked at him. My heart was pounding. I had no idea what he was thinking.

"I can't really tell if you think this is a good thing or a bad thing, Wes."

"It's just, unbelievable. I can't believe it. Are you serious?"

"Yes. Does it make you feel differently about other things?"

"What things?" he asked.

"About me. Does it make you feel differently about me?"

He took a second, staring at me as if searching for words. "No, it doesn't. I'm sorry for my reaction, I'm just shocked."

"Might you still want to take me on a date at Christmas?"

"Might I? Yes, Lila, I very much want to take you on a date at Christmas."

The food came quickly, and it was tasty. Everything tasted better than usual tonight, and I was in the best mood. I loved that he was jealous about the kiss.

Our conversation naturally went to the movie, and we started talking about Anna's high school scene. We talked about my hair and costume, and I told him my approach to her mindset—her outlook on the story.

We talked as we ate. We were so comfortable with each other that we split everything, eating off of each other's plates and each getting to try most of the food. Wes ate more than I did, and I ate a lot. And even after all that, we still had leftovers.

He brought up God again as we slowed down with the food, and we got into a deeper conversation where he asked me specific questions about theology. He was curious about my faith and he seemed open to it. We cleared up the whole thing about my relationship with God not having to do with never kissing a guy.

We were wrapping up that conversation when the waitress came up to ask if we wanted dessert. She seemed excited about the possibility of serving it to us and told us how tasty the sopapillas and the flan were, but we apologized and said we were too full.

It only took us a few minutes to finish up and make our way outside.

"I'll walk you to your car," he said.

I pointed toward the right, and we started heading that way. The weather was nice out, and we walked slowly, meandering in the general direction of my car.

"I was thinking about what happened earlier today in the trailer. You had come up to me just before Gretchen walked in and… you kissed me on the cheek. Would you have been okay if I had…"

I grinned and stared straight ahead, feeling too shy to meet his gaze. He was walking me to my car, and now he was making sure it was okay if we kissed. This was happening. Be still my heart.

"I definitely would have," I said.

"You're telling me you went all these years without kissing a guy, and you would have let it happen two times in one day?"

"I know that sounds absurd, but yes. I didn't mean for it to happen that way. I've wanted it with you, and it's just coincidence that it lines up with Ryder." I said the words casually even though I was nervous.

"You've wanted it to happen with me?" Wes asked, looking at me. I could tell that he had turned to face me even though I wasn't looking his way. I could hear his voice and see him out of the corner of my eye.

Chapter 10

"Did you just say you've wanted it to happen with me?" Wes asked, clarifying.

He was looking at me and I smiled and shrugged as I walked in the parking lot of the Mexican restaurant. Wes started walking backward and leaning down to my line of vision in an effort to get me to look at him.

"Did you say that?" he asked, leaning in front of me.

I stopped walking. We were in the city, and there were people off in the distance, but no one was around us. "I said it," I agreed, nodding. "I have wanted that. I guess it's inappropriate of me to admit since you're my director and we should try to keep it—"

I said nothing else because Wes pulled me into his arms. One second, we were standing in a parking lot, not touching each other at all, and the next, I was in his arms. He stared down at me, and I could feel and see his chest rise and fall as he took a deep breath. He hugged me. I felt him around me and smelled the mint he had just eaten on the way out. The only light was from street lights and the moon, and Wes's dark eyes combined with the color of his shirt made me feel funny inside. I was enamored, spellbound.

"He did it wrong today," he said.

I didn't realize Wes was talking about Ryder until I noticed him looking at me as if he was making a better kissing plan.

"Oh yeah, how so? Are you sure it wasn't my fault? If something was wrong it was probably my fault since it was my first time."

Wes shook his head—a small, almost imperceptible movement that told me experience had nothing to do with it. He licked his lips and I felt an urgency I couldn't explain. I gripped a small piece of his shirt, and he stared at me, looking me over, inspecting my face. He held me and stared at me like he was taking it all in.

"I should have been the first," he said, speaking slowly, quietly. "I cannot believe I could have been the first. And I did this to myself. Maybe it's a kick in the pants by God. I probably deserve it."

"Why would God want to kick you in the pants?" I said. "It meant nothing to me. I was just acting. It was just work."

"And what about this?" he asked. He put his hand on my face, indicating the fact that he was about to kiss me.

"Well, you said it was just business earlier," I said.

"Yeah, but then I changed my mind. I already said I regretted that."

I shrugged, "I mean, you're my director and everything, but it seems like if we're both in agreement about something then it should be okay for us to—you know, since we're both two consenting adults."

"I'm definitely consenting," he said, staring at me.

I grinned. "Then yeah, I mean, we're two consenting adults, like I said."

Wes leaned in and kissed me. He let his perfect lips barely touch mine in a slow, soft kiss where we hardly made contact. It was excruciatingly, gloriously light. The anticipation was out of control. I shook with the effort to stand still and let him come to me, to put his lips on mine.

Wes reached up and took my face into his hands. He cradled me there, pulling back and staring at me like I was some treasure. I smiled at him, feeling like I might melt.

"He should have looked at me like this," I said, blinking and barely getting out the words.

The corner of his mouth rose in an easy grin. "No, he really shouldn't have," Wes said. "It's a good thing, for all of us, that he didn't." He licked his lips again just before he leaned in and kissed me, and my heart ached with the need to get closer. I had never felt compelled to kiss a man before, and now that I was compelled, I felt insane with it. It was like I had been a torch full of oil my whole life, and now I had walked next to an ember. I was lit. My body was on fire, and I desperately wanted to be near Wes and remain there.

He held my head in his hands, staring at me for a second before leaning in to kiss me again. I tasted his peppermint. His mouth was slightly open as he let his lips touch mine, and my blood felt warm and thick. I was aware of my body in a completely new way, and all from his kiss—it was a barely open-mouthed kiss, and it was unbelievable. The act of feeling Wes and tasting him was like nothing I had ever experienced. His mouth was soft and warm, and he gave me three or four of those perfect, soft, lingering kisses.

When he started to break away, I gripped his shirt again, pulling on him, letting him know that I didn't want him to stop. He grinned a little and then it happened again… he kissed me another three or four times before he pulled back, still smiling at me. I let out the breath I had been holding.

"Wes, that was nothiiiing like what happened to me earlier today," I said in a hoarse whisper.

"Good."

He dropped his hands from my face, but he didn't let me go. He grabbed me around the waist, holding me there in the parking lot.

"Wes?"

"Yes."

"Can we please keep all this between us until the movie's finished? I'm really, I'm not scared of Gretchen, but she's pretty intense, and I'd rather not have any kind of confrontation with her." I trailed off and stared at him, hoping he got the idea of what I was trying to say.

"I'm fine with keeping it professional on set, but don't make it about her."

"Okay," I said, even though it was one hundred percent about her.

"I know you need to take things slowly," he said.

As he spoke, I watched the way his mouth moved. I saw his teeth and his tongue as he formed words, and I ached to kiss him again.

What was wrong with me?

"Wes, can I try something?" I asked.

Before he even had time to answer, I leaned in and kissed him again. I opened my mouth and let it soften against him. I used my tongue, and we tasted each other for a gentle few seconds before I pulled back, blinking and staring at him.

"Do you seriously expect me to believe that's the first time you've done this?" he asked, looking serious, staring at me.

"It is, I promise." I was breathless, so I was sure he believed me. "I just watch a lot of daytime television drama. I've been watching it for months. They make out all the time on there. I had a whole plan for how it would feel. I'm not sure how I did because I got nervous, but I told myself I was going to be a good kisser just because of how many soaps I've watched."

Wes stared at me like he was stunned, and then his face broke into a grin. "Are you serious right now? Is this all a big joke?"

"No. I promise, I've never kissed a guy before today."

Neither of us added that I had kissed two of them today. Ryder didn't exist as far as I was concerned. Wes held my hand as we broke apart, and we started walking toward my car, fingers interlocked.

I drove a small, red hatchback, and he knew what it looked like so he headed that way. I was glad Wes had the presence of mind to know how to do normal human things like walk. I could concentrate on nothing besides the kiss we just shared and the fact that he was still holding my hand. I just followed along. Wes held onto me, and I held him back. Holding his hand gave me the oddest mix of feelings. It was completely natural and at the same time new, foreign, and exciting. I felt shaken but so very happy.

"I'm happy we did this," I said at the thought as we approached my car.

Wes pulled me into his arms, moving behind me and hovering over my shoulders for a second. We took a few lumbering steps before he turned me and kissed me again.

We were out there for probably five more minutes. We talked some, but mostly, he kissed me. It was a moment in time that I will never forget. We were standing in a public parking lot, and I was so lost in his presence that it took concentration for me to come back to reality and remember that I needed to be going.

I straightened and pulled back, taking a deep breath and absentmindedly digging in my purse for my keys.

"I am crazy about you, Lila," Wes said. "Say the word, and I will be here waiting for you at Christmas."

"What word do you want me to say?" I asked.

"That you want me."

I grinned and shrugged. "I do happen to want you," I said since I meant it.

"Okay. It's a date, then. Christmas. I'll make a movie, and you'll go to California, and we'll meet back here at Christmas."

"What if I love it over there?"

"Then I'll have to come to California." He was being lighthearted, but I smiled, feeling overjoyed at the thought.

"It seems like we're both going to be a lot less busy at Christmas," I said.

"Yes, but what about before then?" he asked.

I reached out and touched him, running my fingers over his arm absentmindedly. "What about it?" I asked.

"Can you please tell me if you're going out with anyone else?" he asked.

"Are you going to tell me if you're going out with someone else, too?" I asked.

"I'm not going out with anyone else," he said. "I'm telling you that right now."

I made eye contact with him, staring into his dark eyes. I got lost in them. "I'm fine with not going out with anyone else, too," I said.

It was the understatement of the year.

***

I talked to Wes every night on the phone after that. We didn't mean for it to happen that way, but one of us would text the other, and we would end up making a call since it took so long to type everything we wanted to say. We didn't see each other until the following Friday when we filmed Anna's final scene at the local high school.

I hadn't been to a high school in a while, and the familiar sights and smells thrust me into a haze of nostalgia.

Or maybe it was seeing Wes.

I heard bells when Wes was around. Birds chirped and I saw the world in a whole different light—through rose-colored glasses. I was in the best mood when I arrived on set and saw Wes, and I did my best not to make it obvious.

It helped that the scene was heavy. In the movie, Anna's parents passed away tragically, and she was at school when she got the news. She didn't cry, but the scene was all very dramatic, and it took us two hours to film.

Fifty extras had stayed after school to be part of the scene. Wes and Gretchen were both busy, managing all of those people, and I did my best to help them by being ready to work and taking it seriously.

Neither Wes nor I acted on our feelings, but I could tell we both had feelings. We had touched on the subject on the phone, and I could clearly see the way he regarded me when no one was looking at us. That only happened a few times today since we were so busy, but it was enough that I knew his feelings for me existed.

We shot the scene, and then I went into the trailer to take off my microphone. I had been on set, working with Wes for the past few hours, and we had no time alone. I looked up expectantly when I heard the trailer door open, and sure enough, it was Wes.

He stood in the doorway, looking all hard-bodied with masculine energy, and he turned and fastened the lock the instant he came into the door.

I stood up. "Hang on, let me get this thing off," I said, speaking so quietly that I was almost mouthing the words to him.

I fished the small wire out from behind my ear and found the battery pack which was attached to the backside of my undershirt. Wes could see that I was struggling, and he came over to help me. My mic was technically already off, but I felt better after I got the battery pack into my own hand and made sure it was switched off at the source.

Wes had helped me get it off, and now his hand rested lightly on my waist. My heart soared because of it. I had been watching him work all day. I was smitten with him. He had a vision for the movie, and I loved watching his drive and power as he made it come to life. I respected him as a person, and it caused a physical reaction. My body was on fire in the spot where he touched me.

I placed my hand on top of his and turned to face him after I put the mic down.

"You were amazing today," he said.

"Thank you."

"Thank you," he said.

"I haven't seen you in a few days," I said. I popped up and placed a quick, tentative kiss on his mouth, and that caused him to smile and tug on my clothes. He leaned in and kissed me again, this time letting his mouth linger on mine.

The door handle shook.

I jumped back, and it caused him to moan. It was a discontented sound.

"See me tonight," he said quietly.

I nodded. "I'm leaving in two days, so yes. Whenever you can fit it in."

"Tonight," he said.

I nodded again.

"Com-ing!" he announced when the door handle shook again.

Chapter 11

Wes Quinn
Two weeks later

The six-month wait to see Lila at Christmas had just started, and already, it was impossible.

Wes had already caved and arranged to see her. He had a three-day break before the final stretch of shooting flashback scenes, and Wes was using his time off to drive to Arkansas to her family's lake house.

It was only an eight-hour drive to see her, and he knew he had to take advantage of that before she left for California. He had plans to surprise her. They talked every day, and Wes knew details of where she was staying. He easily found it on a map and made reservations for two nights in a nearby lake house. It was still early enough in May that he had no trouble finding one with availability.

Wes did not tell a soul about his plans. He wanted it to be a true surprise. He was fully aware that his unannounced arrival could backfire, but he was relatively sure that wouldn't happen and everything would go smoothly.

He had rented a nice, two-bedroom place, and he unpacked his things and put them inside before getting back into his truck and driving the six miles to the Morgan's house.

Unfortunately, the house he rented did not give him access to a boat. He would have loved to go over there by water, but he had to make the trip in his truck. Wes knew Lila's brother and a few of her family members would be staying at the house, but he had no idea who he would run into first or what they would be doing when he got there. It was mid-afternoon, so there was no telling.

Lila had described the house and even sent him some photos, but he didn't fully know what to expect. He drove past a small house on the property, knowing he was going for something larger, and he was glad he kept driving. He pulled up to a mansion. He parked near a few other vehicles and walked to the closest entrance even though it seemed less formal than the front door.

"Who goes there?" Wes heard the voice over a speaker, and he looked around, searching for a camera—he found one and gave a wave. "State your business, please, sir." It was a man's voice, and he wished it would have been Lila.

"Hello," he said, not sure who he was talking to.

"Blue hat, white shirt. State your business, please, sir."

Wes had on a white t-shirt and a baseball cap, and he smiled. "My name is Wes Quinn. I'm here to see Lila Morgan."

"Lila's my niece. She didn't tell me she was expecting anyone."

"She didn't know, sir. I am here by surprise."

"Okay, I'm down at the dock. Come on down here, and we'll see if we can find Lila together."

"Yes, sir."

Lila had told Wes about her family. She had two uncles who could possibly be at the house, and this one sounded like Max Morgan, the guy who owned the place. Her other uncle was a television producer in Chicago. Wes talked to Lila every day and as far as he knew, neither of her uncles were there. He expected to run into her brother or someone else, but not her uncle. He must have just arrived. Wes would have to roll with it.

He headed toward the lake, which was in clear view from his vantage point near the house. He saw a large dock area. There was a building down there and a couple of nice boats. He saw a man heading toward him from a distance. They both walked with long, confident strides and closed the gap within a minute. Her uncle looked like an older version of the guy who played Aquaman—his long hair pinned half-up and flowing in the wind.

They converged on the lawn near the dock, and both of them used a firm handshake. "I'm Max Morgan, and you said you're Wes Quinn? I haven't heard that name. Where are you from, Wes?" He looked Wes over, sizing him up.

Lila had told Wes a bit about her uncle and his mysterious, formidable, kung-fu-ninja-type ways, but Wes didn't have to be told. He could tell right away that Max Morgan was a take-charge kind of guy.

"Houston," Wes said. "Lila and I made a movie together. My grandfather is a patient of Doctor Morgan, Lila's dad. My grandfather produces General Hospital."

"Oh, I heard Lila's is going out to California for that." Max looked Wes over. "So, you had something to do with that?"

"No, sir. I wish she wasn't going. I'm happy for her, b-but selfishly, I live in Houston, so part of me wishes she was staying there." He shrugged. "Lila had that worked out with my grandfather before she and I met. She stayed in Houston to help me with a small budget film I was directing."

"Why is it small budget if your grandfather owns General Hospital?"

Wes smiled and shrugged. He thought of about ten possible responses and couldn't settle on one of them. He went for complete honesty.

"He gave me some money, and he thinks I lost it, so he's not very happy with me. But he worked with me a little, and Lila is talented. I have a good friend who starred opposite her. It won't look like a low-budget film once we're done with it."

"Did you lose the money?"

"No, sir, but my grandfather doesn't like the way it's tied up. He thinks I lost it."

"What's it tied up in?"

"Renewable energy."

"So, you're an environmentalist indie movie director who doesn't care whether or not his rich grandfather writes him out of the will? Rebel *with* a cause type?"

Wes laughed at the summary. "Yeah, but I do care about the will," Wes said, smiling. "I didn't think I was being careless, but it's up for… we're working it out. I just wanted to be transparent with you because you come across as a… human lie detector."

Max laughed. "Did Lila tell you that?"

"No, sir, she didn't. I kind of wish she would have now that I am in this moment. She said you were in stocks and bonds."

"I am in stocks and bonds." Max looked Wes over. "Does Lila want you here?" he asked.

"Yes, she does. I'm pretty sure she'll be excited to see me."

"Why only pretty sure?"

Wes shrugged. "I am here unannounced. And I've just run into her protective uncle."

Max smiled. "Have I shaken your confidence?" he asked. "I noticed you didn't say *overprotective*. You just said I was protective."

"As far as I've witnessed, you're just being protective."

"Have you met my brother?"

"No, sir, I haven't."

"He's the one who's going to be overprotective," Max said.

Wes stood up straight and smiled at Max. Again, he thought of several things he could say, but couldn't settle on any of them.

"Lila is untarnished by the world," Max said.

"I know," Wes agreed.

"Don't try to tarnish her," Max said.

"I'm not. I'm trying to get her to rub off on me. I love how good she is. I want to protect her from… people… like… me."

"Okay, Wes Quinn, I was going to take you to her anyway, but I actually like you now."

Wes laughed. "Thank you."

"Welcome to our lake house."

"Thank you, it's beautiful out here."

"I just got here an hour ago. I haven't even seen my niece yet. I know she's here because I saw Beck earlier and he told me." Just then Max let out a sharp whistle. "Hey Beck!" he said, shouting a great distance. There was a guy standing near the house and he lifted his arms as if to ask what Max wanted. "Where's Lila?" Max yelled.

"Little Rock!" Beck yelled "Whole Foods!"

Max gestured toward the house, and Wes followed him that way. Beck had been shaking out a rug, and he still held it in his hands as he hesitated by the door, waiting for them. "I'm cleaning my mess," Beck said finally as they approached him.

"What mess?" Max asked.

"The mess of existing," Beck said. "I'm cleaning that blue bathroom. Lila's been gone all day," he continued. "They were doing the grocery store on their way home because they'll have frozen stuff. Do you need her? I can call them if you want… who's this?"

"Who did she go to Little Rock with?" Max asked, skipping over Beck's question.

"Casey. He said something about taking her to some property first—to throw axes and do some target practice with the pistol." Beck said it like he thought he might be mistaken, but Max nodded.

"He mentioned that to me. I didn't know he was taking Lila with him. This is Wes Quinn from Houston."

Beck took a step back, gazing at Wes with a completely different expression. "*The* Wes Quinn? Yes, you sure are. I didn't recognize you with the baseball cap." Beck stared intensely.

"Is Lila going to be interested in seeing this young man?" Max asked.

This caused Beck let out a dazed laugh. "Yeah, sh-she'll want to see him," Beck said, stuttering on purpose as if that were an understatement.

"We can call them and see where they are," Max said. He already had his phone out when he said it.

"Don't tell her he's here," Beck said. "I want to see the look on her face."

Max nodded just as Lila answered her phone. It was on speakerphone. "Hey, my niece, where are you?"

"Hey, Uncle Max. We're almost back, why?"

"I just heard you went to Whole Foods. I was going to try to get you to grab me some of that trail mix I like."

"Oh, no, we left there a while back. We're almost home. I can order you some online, or one of us will be going back before long."

"Yeah, it's fine. Hey, I was just talking to Beck, and he said you have some kind of boyfriend back home."

Beck made a face at him like he was saying too much, and Wes cringed inwardly, having no idea what Lila would say.

"I haven't even seen you and hugged your neck yet, Uncle Max."

"I know but I needed to make sure this guy checks out."

"He checks out," Lila said. "You would like him. He's a weirdo like you."

Both gentlemen looked at each other with wide eyes.

"When do I get to meet him?" Max asked.

"I don't know. Maybe at Christmas. I have to see if I'm coming up here for Christmas this year."

"Lila can shoot!"

Someone on Lila's end of the phone said it. Wes assumed it was Casey, her cousin.

"Oh yeah?" Max asked.

"She's accurate," Casey said. "And she can throw an axe, too."

"Where'd y'all go?" Max asked.

"Out in the woods."

"And you forgot my trail mix? Are you sure you can't turn around?" Max was joking around, and Casey knew it.

"Dad, we're like three minutes from the house," Casey said.

"Okay, I'll see you when you get here." The two of them hung up and Max looked at Wes. "You can park in the garage if you don't want her to see your truck. There's space for another one in there."

The guys barely had time to get Wes's truck into the garage and walk inside when Casey and Lila drove up. They were in her car, but her cousin was driving.

Beck went outside to help them with groceries, and Wes stayed inside with Max. Lila and Beck's mom, Sarah, was there, too. They caught her up on the situation just as Lila came through the door.

Lila was in the process of telling Beck about her shooting experience with Casey. She said she loved shooting at metal because of how gratifying it was when you heard the pinging sound of your target.

Chapter 12

Lila Morgan

"What are you doing in the woods throwing axes like a barbarian?" Beck said, coming outside to meet us when we got back to the lake house.

"I'm going on a soap opera in a week," I said. "Axe throwing might come up. And guns come up on soaps all the time. If I have to hold a gun, it'll be fake, but still, I wanted a lesson from Casey about how to do it."

"Lila's a natural with a gun," Casey said. "I want her on my team in a zombie apocalypse. She shot four different guns, and she hit targets with all of them."

"Aw, shucks," I said, hefting a paper bag full of groceries into my arms. "We're still going to have to make two trips," I added when I looked at the five or six bags of food. "Plus, there are two coolers in my trunk."

"Let's just get the bags inside, and we can get the coolers in a minute," Beck said. He looked at me as he picked up two bags and we headed to the house. "So, you wanted to learn to shoot for the soap opera?"

"Yeah, why not?" I said. "I'm trying to learn anything I can just in case I have to do it when I'm acting. Casey's an expert with guns. He was showing me just how to hold each of them. You know that thing where they put the gun to the side in action movies, that's totally fake."

My brother held the door open for me and I walked past him, heading into the house.

"Did you hit a target?" Beck asked.

"All of them," Casey said.

"I like the metal ones because of that sound they make," I said. "They ping."

I crossed to the kitchen with the two bags I was holding. I gently set them on the counter. They had been heavy, and I was glad to make it inside. I looked up at the people in the room. Everyone seemed to be looking at me. My uncle Max was there. My mother was there, too, and another person who I thought was my cousin, Charlie. My eyes roamed over this person, and I almost choked when I saw his face.

"W-wes?" I felt weak in the knees. I felt weak everywhere. I thought I might pass out. I had the oddest sensation that I was in a dream, and it seemed to take four centuries to cross over to him.

My heart pounded so violently that my ears rang. I could not get to Wes fast enough. I felt as though I was tripping over myself even though I wasn't. I could not breathe until I was in his arms. I went to him as fast as I could. I vaguely heard my family members react about the speed at which I crossed the room.

Wes was wearing a baseball cap. I had never seen him in one of those, and he looked handsome and sporty. I approached him, smiling and trying to hold back tears. I prayed that this wasn't a dream or vision because I did not stop or lessen my momentum. I trusted him to catch me. I thrust myself into his arms. I could not look at him. I could not pick my head up. I fell into his arms and I stuck to him like I was made of magnets and he was metal. I squeezed him, resting my face on his chest.

"Oh my gosh, what are you doing here?"

"This is Wes," my uncle Max said. "I guess you know him already."

"I so know him," I said. "What are you doing here? I thought you were filming. How did you get here? When did you get here?"

I held onto him, not daring to pick my face up off of his chest or look at him. I was aware of the fact that my family went on talking to each other in an effort to give us some privacy. Finally, I pulled back, smiling as I made eye contact with Wes.

"I drove," he said. "I have my truck with me. I parked it in the garage just now so I could surprise you."

"You *did* surprise me," I said, shaking as I held onto him. "You drove all the way over here?"

"Yeah, I left this morning. You were right. It's not that bad. I'll stay tonight and tomorrow and head back early on Sunday."

"Are you staying with me? I mean, here, at this house?"

"No, I rented a house. It's just a few miles from here."

"Two nights?" I asked.

He nodded, but he stood up straight and kept his expression fairly neutral. We were right in the middle of my family. They were doing their best to give us space, but we were in a common area and they were still standing and mingling all around us.

I kissed Wes on the cheek and then took him by the hand and turned with him so that he could meet my mom and the rest of my family.

We spent some time with my family. We talked continuously as we put up the groceries, and then we sat around the kitchen and living room, and two hours passed in a heartbeat. Before I knew it, we were talking about what we were going to eat for dinner.

We voted for getting takeout from a little restaurant that was fifteen miles away, and Uncle Max volunteered to go get the food while the rest of us stayed back. Wes and I had laid off the physical contact while he was getting to know my family, but I missed him so much these last few weeks, and I was aching to be close to him.

"Do you want to swim later?" I asked, knowing I could at least accidentally brush up against him if we were in the pool.

"I'd love to, anytime," he said. "I figured we would. Are you talking about the lake or the pool?"

"I was thinking the pool," I said.

"Let's go now," he said, looking me over casually.

"You've been driving all day," I said. "I'll bet it would feel good to swim." I looked at the clock. "We have at least thirty minutes before the food gets back." I glanced down at his shorts, which conveniently were fit for swimming. "We're going swimming!" I added, announcing it to everyone else.

I stopped at the closet to get towels, and Wes was in the pool by the time I got outside. My mom had made her way to the patio, but she was near the house and preoccupied with her iPad. I set our towels on a chair by the side of the pool and took off my shorts and t-shirt, getting down to my swimsuit. It was a modest one-piece, and I still felt vulnerable enough that I jogged to the pool.

"Be careful," I heard Wes warn as I ran, and I smiled at the sound of his voice. I was being careful, but I made it to the pool quickly and I jumped straight in without hesitation. I strategically landed in the four-foot area where I went into the water up to my chest, keeping my head dry.

Wes had already gone under. His face and hair were wet. My hair was in a ponytail and completely dry. I glanced at my mom who was not looking at us, and then I swam toward Wes and didn't stop until I met up with him and kissed his mouth.

"Mm, you taste like candy," he said, holding onto me under the water. He spoke in a quiet tone that no one but me could hear.

"I ate a lifesaver," I said, equally as quietly.

There was a dish full of them on the counter. We had both seen them.

"What color?" he asked.

"Purple."

"Grape?"

"Yep."

"Mmm," he said again, causing both of us to smile.

I kissed him again and then reached and held onto him under the water. "I was missing you so much," I said, still speaking quietly.

He pulled me toward the deep end, and I went to him, holding onto him and going into the water up to my shoulders.

"We have a lot of room at this house," I said. "You could stay in a whole separate house from me and still stay here. My family would be fine with it."

"Thank you, but I already reserved that place. My stuff is over there. I'll stay late and then come back in the morning."

"That's right. Sunrise. What time?"

(We had already talked about getting together the following morning for sunrise.)

"I'll come over early. I'll come wake you up."

His hair was even darker now that it was wet. It was cut short on the sides, but the top was longer and it hung in careless wet waves over his forehead. His dark eyes seemed to look straight into my heart. I stared at him as we both floated in the water.

I reached up and expertly took my hair out of the ponytail holder. I shook my head before leaning back and going under the water for the first time. I came up and opened my eyes, blinking to find Wes smiling at me.

We kissed again, but I knew my family could see us, so we were light and quick with it. "I'll see you in Texas before you head out in a couple of weeks," he said.

"Yeah, and then it might be a while," I said.

I would have my hands full with moving and trying to make my way in California, and Wes would have his hands full with editing the movie. I held onto his arms underwater.

"I feel sad about it," I said. "I'm happy for each of us, and I like our respective goals, but my heart is happy when you're next to me. I miss you when you're not with me."

Wes put his hand on my waist. "You have no idea," he said. "Things are way better for me when I can reach out and touch you, Lila."

I stood there in the water and held onto him for a minute or two. It felt good to just chill in each other's presence and make light physical contact under the cover of the water. With his shirt off, I could see the shapes and lines of his body through the clear water. I was in love, and I was so thankful he was willing to come here to see me.

"Where did you tell everyone you were going?"

"Out of town," he said.

"You got away with being that vague about it?" I asked. "With Gretchen?"

I knew they were working closely together during this movie. She was helping him with a lot of the responsibility.

"I told her I was going out of town to see a friend. I didn't know what you would want me to say to her."

"It's not about me," I said. "It's you who needs her. You don't want to ruffle her feathers.

"Lila, look at me," Wes said.

I glanced at him.

"Does it make you sad that I'm working with Gretchen?"

"No, it's not that. She's good at what she's doing, and she's helping you. I just wish she was cool with us, you know? But she'd never be cool with it. The thing is, I sympathize with her. I'd be ready to fight if someone else came in here and started trying to steal you away from me."

"You didn't steal me from Gretchen. I was never with her. I'm glad you'd fight if you had to, though. What style of fighting would you do?"

"Any," I said. "Whatever I have to do. Right now, I have to deal with months away from you. That feels like a fight in itself. Gretchen doesn't know we're dating and we should probably keep it that way."

"I'm happy to tell Gretchen we're dating. I almost told her I was coming up here, but I didn't say anything for your sake. If you want me to, I'll easily tell her we're together. I thought we were just keeping it lowkey until the movie release."

"Yeah, that's what I'm saying. We should keep it lowkey so she'll keep helping you with the movie."

"No," he said.

"No, what?"

"Don't put it like that. I'm not keeping this a secret just to get Gretchen to help me. I can do it without her if she can't handle us being together."

"Wes, thank you, really, thank you for saying that and for being willing to tell her… but no. It would change everything in your dynamic."

"Nothing is going on between me and Gretchen," he said.

"I know, but she thinks there's the possibility."

"Yeah, but that's not right. That implies that I'm leading her on."

"I know you're not, but Wes, I also know that it's not wise to go breaking her heart if you don't have to. She's helping you a lot."

He tilted his head, studying my face. "Can we not talk about Gretchen?" he asked.

I smiled at him as we held hands under the water. "I would love that. Let's talk about what we're going to do for the next two days," I said.

"I'll just wait on you to tell me where to go."

"Swim, dinner, maybe another swim. There's a tire swing and a hammock—we can go for a walk in the woods, watch a movie, snuggle on a couch, sleep, wake up, go out on the lake and watch the sunrise, eat breakfast, maybe a hike to a waterfall or something fun and nature-y tomorrow. Of course, we'll have food and swimming."

We were speaking so quietly that there was no way my mom overheard us.

"I am so glad I came," he said.

I held onto him. "I'm glad you came, too," I said.

Chapter 13

Four months later
Los Angeles, California

It was September in Los Angeles, but I spent so much time inside a television studio that I hardly noticed what month it was or what the weather was like.

My father's upbringing made me an overachiever, and I found myself in a position where I was working with the directors, staying late, and doing what I could to help around the set on General Hospital. I wasn't doing it to be a brown-noser, but it worked out that they really liked me because of it.

I was having fun and fitting in, and I was already getting the feeling that I would be worked into a larger role one day. Even if things didn't pan out with General Hospital, I was making friends and professional relationships in Hollywood that would translate to future work.

I had called in a favor to get my foot in the door, but I wasn't afraid of working hard. I had only been out there for a short while, and I was already gaining confidence and momentum.

I was in a routine with Wes also. He and I were still in a long-distance relationship. We talked every day, and we last saw each other a month ago when he came to California for a short visit.

Wes Quinn was my one and only. We were both busy with our own projects and endeavors, but we were important to each other, and we definitely had plans to be together after the first of the year even though we weren't sure where or how that would work out.

Wes had some setbacks in the editing process lately, and we spent some of our time on the phone talking about his project. After being here and working with these people, I really appreciated how much he had gotten done with how little he had to work with. I loved Wesley Quinn, and I couldn't wait until we were both less busy and we could live in the same city and be together. I was proud of him and proud of the movie.

It was Friday afternoon, and I picked up my phone, smiling when I saw it was Wes.

"Hey," I said. "What are you doing?"

"I'm just leaving the office. I was working, but I'm going to get something to eat. What about you?"

"I am just leaving the studio," I said. "I'm supposed to meet some people from the show tomorrow morning. We're all going for a hike. Can you believe it?"

"A hike? That sounds… healthy."

"I know," I said, laughing reluctantly. "I'm a little scared."

"Just take water."

"I am. Two bottles. One for water, and one for iced coffee."

He laughed.

"What are you doing in the morning? Are you going to the gym?"

"No, I actually have a meeting with a couple of actresses."

"Actresses? For what?"

"I, uh, you know. I've been having trouble with Gretchen not showing up and stuff."

"Yeah."

"Well, now she's completely out of the picture. I'm meeting with actresses to play that mom role to see if we can reshoot those five scenes."

"Reshoot? What are you saying, Wes?"

"Gretchen. She's done. She had been hard to work with for a while, but now she's done. She said she wanted completely out of the movie. We're reshooting those scenes where she played Anna's mom. I thought about cutting them, but they're crucial. In the morning, I'm going to meet with a few people who I can afford, and I'll see if I think we can pull it off."

"Wait a second, you're telling me you have to *reshoot* multiple scenes of the movie? You have to get *everybody together* and reshoot with someone else playing Anna's mom?"

"Yes. Exactly."

"How long ago did Gretchen quit, Wes?"

"It's been going down for a while, but we had a final conversation the other day, and she called me back afterward and told me she wanted nothing to do with the film—she wanted her part to be taken out of it."

"Was she holding that over your head?"

"Yes, she was."

"Was it about me?"

"No."

"It was, wasn't it? Why didn't you tell me this was happening?"

"Because I didn't want you to think it was your fault."

"Wes, this is a huge blow for your movie. I had no idea you were having trouble with Gretchen. Why didn't you tell me?"

"Because I didn't want you to worry about it. There was nothing you could do. I was covering it. It wasn't that big of a deal until she said she wanted her scenes cut."

"This is a huge deal for you. I am so sorry. How long has she been flaking out on you?"

"A while. I've gotten used to not having her around."

"Was it you coming to California that did it? Did that trip make her stop helping you?"

I heard him take a deep breath. "Lila, I can hear it in your voice. I knew you were going to do this. I knew you were going to start worrying about it. That's why I didn't want to tell you."

"I can't believe you kept it from me."

"I didn't *keep it* from you. It's not like it was a secret. I hoped to just leave her scenes in it and not bother you with worrying about her quitting, but I'm not going to lie to you about having to reshoot scenes. I know you care about me, and I knew it would hinder you to learn that I was struggling."

"Are you struggling?"

"No. It is what it is. At this point, I think I'll try to push back the release date and get someone else to star in that role of Christine. It's not the end of the world if the release date gets pushed back, and I think the film would suffer without her in there. Things happen. I'm trying to roll with it."

"I'm so sorry, Wes. Just tell me… did she leave you because you came to California to see me?"

"That wasn't the problem. The problem was that she was convinced I could be talked into a relationship, but then she finally understood that I couldn't. She got her feelings hurt when it all came to a head, but I wasn't interested in her like that, so ultimately, she said she couldn't look at me ever again."

"I am so sorry, Wes."

"Don't be. I didn't want you to be sorry. I'd rather take her out of the movie if she's going to be like that. It sucks having to reshoot, but I don't really care. I'd rather go through it than have her in the film. I coached her through that role, I can do it for somebody else. I feel like I'm going to be able to work with this woman tomorrow. I talked to her on the phone, and she seems really nice—and from her headshot, she's close enough. It's just a matter of getting everyone together and redoing it. But I did it once, I can do it again."

My mom had called while Wes was talking, and it distracted me for a second, but this was too big of a deal for me to answer. I could call my mom back later.

I knew Wes would have a much harder time scheduling and executing those scenes without Gretchen's help. She managed a lot for him, and I felt sick at the thought of him trying to redo so much of the movie without her.

"You can do it again, and I'm so proud of you, but geez, Wes, I am so sorry she left you in a bind like that."

"Thank you, but I'll make it."

"What about her name in the credits?" I asked.

"She doesn't want anything to do with the film."

I breathed a long sigh, not knowing what to say. I hated this news, but I knew he didn't want me to make a big deal about it. "Please let me know if there's something I can do to help you, Wes. Seriously I'll make phone calls or schedule things for you or whatever you need. I can do a lot from over here."

"Thank you very much, my love, but you have your own things going. I'll handle it. I was just letting you know about the change in plans."

I talked with Wes on the phone for another hour before letting him go. My mom had called twice during that time, so I called her back when I got off the phone with him.

"Hello?"

"Hey, Mom, you called?"

"Yeah, did you get my message?"

"No, I just saw that you called and called you back. Is everything okay?"

"Yeah, I was just looking through old photographs. Are you still seeing Frank Quinn's grandson long distance?"

"Yes, big time. In fact, oh my goodness, Mom, I just got off the phone with him, and I'm so torn…"

"Torn about what?"

"Coming home. I want to go to him. I feel like I want to go to Wes and help him. I'm here, and it's fun and I'm meeting people, but for what? He needs me right now with this movie. I was thinking I could play the role of Christine. I could do it. I would be perfect for it. I have a friend at the show who does hair and makeup. She loves special effects. She and her husband both get into it. They could make me look different enough to play my own mom."

"Lila, I got lost a while back. I'm not sure what you're talking about."

"Wes. He needs me for this movie again. He's going to be overwhelmed with all the stuff Gretchen used to do."

"Someone quit? Can't he just hire someone else?"

"Maybe. But not someone who could do the things I can do. I don't mean to sound full of myself, but I'm invested in the project, emotionally. I want it to be great. And so, no, he couldn't hire someone like me."

"What are you saying?"

"I don't know what I'm saying. I feel like I need to leave California and go over there. I feel like I'm going to be needed on this project for the next two or three months until he gets it out. I don't know what that will mean for General Hospital. At this point, I'm just an extra in the scenes, so I'm not really worried about leaving them. They won't be in a bind at all."

"So, that's it? You're just picking up and leaving California? Before you've even heard what I called to tell you?"

"What do you mean what you called to tell me? Do you have something to say?"

"Yes. About Wes."

"About Wes? Why haven't you said it already?"

Chapter 14

I called Wes later that night. I was full of excitement, expectancy, and purpose. A lot had shifted in my life during the last few hours—a lot had changed in my mind and heart, and I felt dazed by it. But at the same time, I was confident and at peace, and I knew I was making the right decision.

"My baby," I said sweetly to Wes when he picked up the phone.

"Yeah, what about it?" he asked slowly, a smile in his voice.

"I'm going to tell you a story, and then I'm going to FaceTime you. I have some big things to tell you and ask you."

"Whoa. This doesn't sound like a normal phone call."

"It's anything but normal. I have thought about nothing but this since I hung up the phone with you."

"What? Whoa, now I'm really interested."

"Let me just start by telling you the story about my mom. This is unbelievable, Wes. Are you somewhere comfortable?"

"Yes, what? Yes, I'm comfortable."

"I can't even believe it, considering our whole history with the storyline of the movie and everything I can't even believe I'm telling you this."

"Lila, what is it?"

"I was already thinking about taking matters into my own hands when I got off the phone with you earlier, but then, my mom told me this unbelievable story and I… let me back up. I hung up the phone with you a while ago, and I called my mom. I had two missed calls from her, so I called her back. She was looking at old photographs, and she had this picture of me when I was a little kid. She said she was at a fundraiser. First of all, let me just say that I know it's you in it with me. My mom didn't know if it was you, but I know it's you. It's the craziest thing, Wes. You came up in my childhood. Just like your movie. It's Full Circle, just like the movie. I remember you. It was one of my earliest memories. I look at that picture, and I should have been too young to even remember, but it was one of the most memorable things I ever did. I hardly ever got in trouble, and I got in trouble for this, so it stuck in my mind. I remember doing it, and getting in trouble, Wes. If it's you in the picture it's going to be the most amazing thing that's ever happened in the whole world. It's going to be just like your movie. We would have to, I don't know, call the news or something."

"Lila do you have a picture of me and you together when we were babies? Is that what you're saying? I can hardly hear you, and I'm trying to piece this together."

I put the phone more securely on my ear. "Yes. It's not just a picture, but actual memories—I have actual memories of you. You are band-aid boy in my stories."

"What?"

"I'm almost sure it's you, Wes, and if it is... okay. My mom called. She thought about an old picture, this one of me with a little boy my age, about a year younger, which makes sense. He and I were in the children's area of some function our parents were doing. He was crying, and I used a *whole box* of band-aids. He and I went off to a corner and one by one, I peeled and stuck them all over this little boy—his legs and arms, and head. I remember sticking them to his hair. I remember being so proud of myself and then getting in big trouble when the adults saw us. I remember that picture my mom had. I looked at it as an older child, and I recalled sticking bandages all over this other kid. I don't know who took the picture. I just know I stuck them on a boy, and then got in trouble. It's something that came up several times in my childhood, though. My dad even brought it up when he was trying to talk me into going to medical school."

"And you think it was *me* you stuck bandages on?"

"I'm pretty sure it is. Wouldn't that be insane? That's why my mom called me. She remembered meeting someone at that function who said they opened a coffee shop and named it after their son. She said she put all the pieces together earlier today and remembered that photograph. She dug it up and texted me the photo."

"So, you have the photo?"

"Yes."

"And you think it's us?"

"Yes. I do. And it makes sense, age-wise, and with us both being raised in Houston. I'm about four or so, and you look a little younger—two-and-a-half. My mom said she doesn't remember who took it. She said it was with others from that function, so she or my dad must have taken it. I remember doing it, though, Wes. I remember putting bandages all over a boy. It's one of my first memories of my whole life. Just like your movie. Isn't that the craziest thing you've ever heard? It was you, I think."

"How sure are you that it's me in the picture?" he asked.

"I don't know. It looks like you, but you're a baby. My mom said she thinks she met your parents at that same function where I did that."

"What about you?"

"I think it's you, Wes. I think you're band-aid boy. I'm texting you the picture right now. Tell me what you think."

I heard the sound when my text went through and then I sat there, waiting to hear what he would say. He was quiet for several long seconds.

"Did it come through?" I asked.

"Yeah, it did," he said.

"Do you think it's you?"

"Is that you?" he asked. "In the pink dress?"

"Yes. That's me." I stared down at the old picture on my phone as I talked to Wes on speaker phone. "Is that you?" I asked.

There was a red-faced toddler with what must've been thirty band-aids all over his body and face. They were the tan, plastic ones, and I had flashes of memories of taking the paper backing off of each one before I stuck them to him. It made him stop crying, so technically it worked.

"That's me, Lila."

He was quiet after he said it.

"It's unbelievable, isn't it?"

"I'm sitting here, looking at it, and it's completely unbelievable." His words were slow and sincere, and I could picture him staring at the photo.

I wished I was there to see him and give him this news in person. "I miss you," I said at the thought.

"I miss you, too," Wes said. "Is this really you in this picture?"

"Yes, I remember doing that to you, Wes. I cannot believe that's you."

"We have to have it framed," he said.

"We have to *at least* have it framed. We might have to have it painted or something like that. But that's not all I'm calling to tell you."

"What is it?"

"I'm at it again."

"You're at *what* again?" he asked.

"Applying bandages."

"You're going back to medical school? Are you coming back home?"

"Yes, but not for medical school. I was already thinking about doing this before my mom called with that picture, and that just sealed the deal. I need you to call me. I mean, FaceTime. Can you do that right now?"

"Yeah, hang on, I'll call you back."

We hung up, and within a matter of seconds, his FaceTime call came in.

I answered, aiming the camera at my own face and making sure he could see me.

"Whoa, hello? What is this? Who are you?" he asked, looking confused.

"I know, right? I mean. Can you believe it? Isn't it amazing? My friend, Nicole, at the show came over and did it for me just now. She's been over here for the last two hours. She gave me the pieces and taught me how to do it and everything. I think I have to get some more glue, but it's easy to find. If not, I can hire someone to help me."

"Are you my girlfriend?" Wes asked, staring at the screen intently. "You sound like Lila."

"Yes, Wes. It's me." I peered at this handsome face on the screen. "I miss you," I said.

I had a small prosthetic attached to my cheeks and the bridge of my nose, and I had my makeup done just right that I looked similar to me, but also not like me at all. I had also styled my hair differently on purpose.

"I'm auditioning for the role of Christine, Anna's mom. I know you have someone auditioning in the morning, but I think I can beat her out. I have all of Christine's lines memorized—pretty much. I'd like to read any of it for you. Is there a certain section you'd like to hear?"

"What are you doing, you big goofball?"

"I'm not being a goofball. I'm being serious. Do you think I could get away with playing Anna's mom in this?" I gestured to my face. "My friend helped me do this. Isn't it amazing? She told me what to do. I'll be able to re-create it."

"It is amazing and it's wonderful. If you were here, you would have the role in a heartbeat."

"That's what I'm trying to say to you. I'm coming home. I mean, if you want me to. If you'll have me. I want to play that role. I know I can do it. I tried it, and I know I can pull it off. I even change my voice."

"That would actually be amazing," he said. "If you come home for a few days, I could try to schedule everything where we film the scenes back-to-back. I could try to get them shot in a matter of a few days if I schedule everything perfectly."

"No, I'm coming home indefinitely. I'm helping you with scheduling and everything. I'm just in the background fake-taking blood pressure over here. I want to go home. I want to be with you. Honestly, I just want to come home and help you even if you don't hire me for the role of Anna's mom. I don't need to play her. I just thought it might work since I already look like Anna."

"I want you," he said. "I want anything you're saying right now. I want you to play Christine, and I also want you to come home. I don't want you to leave Hollywood if that's your dream, but I'm also going to hightail it to California and get you if you say you want to come home."

"I want to come home," I said. "I can't wait to. Do you need to see my audition?"

"No, I don't, my precious love. You will be great. You will be brilliant. The movie is going to be amazing because of you, I can just feel it. You're going to be a big star."

"You're going to be a big star director."

"I don't need that."

"Why not?"

"That's not what I set out to do. I was searching for anything when I wrote that script. I remembered seeing that birth in real life, and I just wrote my variation of it."

"Everybody gets inspiration from somewhere," I said.

"I really only did it to earn my grandfather's respect. I don't care about the money he may or may not give me one day. I just hoped I could take a little and make a lot in the field he's been in all these years. I thought if I could do that, he'd think I was a capable human."

"You are a capable human, Wes. You're more than capable. The movie is going to be a total hit."

"Yeah, well, whatever happens with the movie is extra because I already won. I beat the game."

"What's that mean?"

"I won. In life. I have you."

"Are you saying being with me is beating the game of life?" I asked.

"I am saying exactly that, Lila," he said.

Those words caused chills to go up my spine. I could not wait to go to him. I knew I was doing the right thing. I needed to go to him. General Hospital would be there when we were done with the movie. Or it wouldn't. I would make something else happen. But for now, I knew what I had to do. I had to go back to Houston.

"When can you come pick me up?" I asked.

"Whenever you're ready."

Chapter 15

Three weeks later
Houston, Texas

Today had been a long day, and the next few days would be even longer, but it would all be worth it.

We had just finished day one of reshooting, and we came to Wes's office to drop some things off and download files to his main computer. Wes had a big, sturdy, wooden desk, and I sat on it while he worked on his computer for a minute. He turned to me and smiled once the files started downloading. He held me and rested his head on my leg, letting out a relieved sigh.

"I cannot wait to go through this footage. It's so much better than the last time. I've gotten better at shooting it, and you're such a better Christine. This whole thing was a blessing in disguise."

I ran my fingertips through the hair on his hairline.

"I'm so glad you had that woman there to help you with your face," he said.

We had hired a makeup artist to help me transform into Christine. I could have never done it on my own. I had enough on my plate with becoming Christine in other ways. I wanted to make her different from Anna in subtle, not forced ways. I changed my gate and my posture just slightly, and I spoke in a lower tone. In the past few weeks, I had been consumed with becoming Christine in voice and mannerisms. I worked hard at it, and that translated to me becoming her for hours each day as I practiced and perfected her vibe.

I wouldn't consider myself the most naturally talented actress that had ever been born. But I absolutely knew the importance of hard work, and I wasn't afraid of it. I poured time into Christine and by the time we shot the scene today, I felt like I was prepared and I went out there and nailed it.

"I could have never pulled that makeup off by myself," I said. "She has me looking even better than the first day I wore it."

"It looked amazing," Wes agreed tiredly. "You were unbelievable today. We'll be done in two days if the rest of it goes like it did today."

"Samantha was great, too," I said, referring to the little girl who played young Anna.

"Everything went smoother than it did last time," he said, nodding. "It took us three days last time to get the footage we got today."

"Well, it was a long day," I said.

"Yeah, but productive. Thank you," he said, holding onto my legs like they were a pillow. "Thank you for everything. I would not be in a good position with the movie right now if you didn't come back home."

I rubbed his back. "We're a good team," I said.

I wanted to tell him I loved him, but we hadn't said it yet. I felt it and I knew Wes felt it, but we hadn't said it. We sat quietly in each other's presence for a moment while the computer did its thing.

An odd pinging sound happened, and Wes turned and sat up regarding the computer screen. He clicked a button and the screen showed security footage from the elevator.

Gretchen was in it, and Wes sat up and looked at me. "I get a notification when someone pushes this floor on the elevator."

"That's live? Is she coming up here right now?"

"I can get up and lock my office door, but she might still see us in here. I don't think I have time to make it to the elevator and… I'm stuck," he added, standing up since Gretchen was about to get off of the elevator on our floor. "At this point, I have to talk to her because she's going to see me if I walk over to lock the door. I'll go ask her to leave." He started to head to his door.

"I'm hiding," I whispered. "I don't want to talk to her or deal with her at all. I'm going in here."

I moved quickly. There was a closet in his office, and I ran to it, feeling nervous and shaken like I was hiding from a gang of approaching villains in an action movie. The minute I closed the door, I began doubting myself and thinking I should have stayed out there with Wes.

Part of me was relieved to not be out there, but I had no idea if I made the right choice. I wasn't normally a hide-in-a-closet type of person. I sank my head into my hand and took a deep, calming breath. I reminded myself that I was in control of my own destiny and then I could just walk out of the closet at any time.

I was having that thought when I heard Gretchen speaking. They were on the other side of the room, so it was quiet, but I could hear her.

"I heard you re-shot my scene today," she said.

"We re-shot Christine's scene, yes."

"I talked to Samantha's mom and she said you had Lila Morgan out there, putting stuff all over her face and trying to play multiple roles."

"She is doing that," he agreed. "She's helping me out."

"Don't be cheap, Wes. It's not that kind of movie. Nobody wants to see a Tyler Perry in your indie film. It's an art piece. Don't cheapen it. I would feel terrible if I let you sell the whole thing short by using her."

"You really shouldn't feel terrible, Gretchen. Nothing is compromised. I love the footage we got today. I'm fine. The movie's fine."

"That's why I'm coming here!" she barked, somewhat frantically. The words came out as if she was in a hurry. It seemed like he might be ushering her off, and she was trying to stay. "The movie's not fine. You're not fine. Don't do this to your movie. (She was crying.) Just use the footage you have of me. I'm sorry I made you waste today, but at least you don't have to do any more reshooting. Save your money, and use the footage you have. I was just hurt because I love you, Wes. But I love you too much to see you do this to your movie. Just use the footage of me."

"Gretchen, thank you, but I like the footage we got today better for a number of reasons. Lila is just one of them."

"You're settling for that," she said. "Don't settle."

"I'm not settling," he said. "I'm happier with multiple aspects of the footage from today."

"Then let's reshoot it with me playing Christine. We'll get it right. I want to do it for you, Wes. I love you too much to leave you in a bind like this."

"You left me in a bind weeks ago, Gretchen. I've already recovered from the bind you left me in. I'm no longer in that bind. Thank you for reconsidering and for coming by, but you need to be going. I have work to do."

"Don't do this, Wes. I'm here and I'm willing, and I'm the one who loves you. I'm the one who's always waiting around when you come back to Houston. That girl won't wait around. She already left you once."

"Gretchen, I need you to go ahead and leave before you say things that make me upset."

"Oh, *you're* upset? God forbid *you* be upset! How do you think I feel? You're sitting here telling me you'd rather use footage of a girl dressed up and playing two characters than footage of me."

"I'm sorry if that makes you upset, Gretchen, but it's the truth. You need to go."

"Or what?"

"Or I will call someone to come walk you down."

"This is not how this meeting should go, Wes. (She was crying again.) I am *freely giving* my time to you. Just like I already did for so much of this movie. I'm telling you that I'll do whatever you need or want. I'll learn the part just like you want it. I'll play Christine ten times better than her. It's not good having the same person play two roles in the movie. That's second-rate, and you know it."

"It's not your movie, though, Gretchen."

"Please, Wes, listen to me!" she said it in a loud, begging tone that caused me to flinch.

Multiple times during this conversation, I had been tempted to open the door and walk out there. I was tempted to right now. I didn't stay in the closet because I was afraid. I stayed because I wanted to let Wes deal with it without interfering. I thought it would embarrass him to have a woman come out of a closet in the middle of an awkward conversation. I didn't want to be a part of that kind of scene, so there I was, in a closet with nothing to do but listen to them and this hideous conversation.

"Just please listen to me," Gretchen added in a calmer tone than before. "I don't ask you for much, Wes, but I'm asking you to please reconsider this decision. Think of our past. We have history together. You can't tell me you're going to throw away this relationship *and* this movie over this girl."

"The girl you're referring to, Gretchen, makes the movie better."

"You can't really think that. You're just saying it to try to get a rise out of me."

"I'm definitely not doing that," Wes said calmly. "Listen, Gretchen, I thought you were my friend, and then you left me in a bind. I made it by without you, and I'm doing good now. I'm sorry you changed your mind, but you can't expect me to change mine. You left, and I moved on."

"*I would never have left if you would have just loved me!*" She screamed, almost roaring the words.

"You have to go, Gretchen."

"You have to go, Gretchen," she said mimicking him. "You're going to regret this," she added. It sounded like she was leaving.

"What do you mean by that?" he asked, sounding serious.

"You're going to regret it for the movie and for yourself, Wes. You're never going to get satisfied by little miss perfect. She's not going to be able to do the things I…"

Do the things she what? I thought.

But that was the last thing I heard them say. I heard their voices as they continued to talk, but the sounds got further and further from me as if he was following her out of the room. I sat there in the closet for all of three seconds before I cracked the door open. The two of them were already retreating toward the elevator. I saw their backs as they walked off.

The computer was still switched to the security cameras, and I watched as they got into the elevator together. I couldn't hear what they were saying, but I could see them going back and forth. I knew enough about computers to have easily found and adjusted the volume, but I didn't want to hear what they were saying.

Gretchen had already done enough damage with her Tyler Perry remarks. I took it personally at first, and then I realized how successful Tyler Perry was, and I thought she must think I'm pretty good if she even compared me to him. I had to be in a certain league for her to bring up his name in comparison to me. Christine was a serious role and Gretchen may have been meaning to cut me down when she brought up a comedian, but I was able to mentally shift her remarks into a compliment.

I also loved how Wes had handled her. He was still making me smile as they rode in the elevator and he spoke and scowled at her. She was crying, and I could tell he was not budging, and it made me feel happy. The elevator opened. It stayed open for a while, and they said some other things, but eventually, she got off while he stayed on.

Wes glanced at the camera when the door closed, but he had no idea I was watching. He was alone, and he was headed my way. I was completely in love. He was a sight to behold as he propped himself in the corner of the elevator.

Chapter 16

Six months later
MTV Studios, Los Angeles, California

MTV's Indie Pulse
Backstage

"For God has not given us the spirit of fear, but of power and of love and a sound mind. A sound mind. Power and love. He hasn't given me fear. He gives me power. Power and a sound mind. I'm good. I'm powerful. I'm sound. I can do this through His power. I have a sound mind."

I whispered those words so quietly that most of them were inaudible. I was mumbling some of the time as I kept repeating the scriptural affirmation.

I heard a tap on my dressing room door.

"Come in," I said, probably too quickly.

I stared at the door, thinking it would be one of the producers giving me a last call before they took me to the stage.

But it wasn't.

"Oh, thank goodness you're here," I said. I'd been sitting at the vanity, and I stood up and turned to Wes, walking straight into his arms.

I hadn't seen him in a week, and it felt like longer. I had been missing him something awful, and I was so anxious for him to arrive that it felt like an actual weight had been lifted off my chest now that he was there.

"What happened?" I asked, since he barely made it to the studio in time for the interview.

"My flight was delayed," he said, kissing the side of my forehead. "I missed you, too. You look beautiful."

"Knock, knock, we're coming in!" Someone announced from the door as they opened it.

Two ladies came inside. One was the producer, Kat, and one was the hair and makeup person. I had already met them both.

"Okay, so it looks like you made it in time, Mr. Quinn. Brad will be interviewing you instead of Ms. Morgan. We're going with the same questions we went over via email. We'll just ask you about the movie—your inspiration, where people can watch it, and things like that. Your segment will last approximately ten minutes."

"All right," Wes replied calmly.

The hair and makeup person was already working on Wes. He sat in the chair, calmly listening to Kat and letting the makeup lady do what she needed to do to prepare him for being on the show. Kat hooked a wireless microphone to his shirt and told him it wouldn't be switched on until he went on stage.

"The show has already started. Brad's out there with his first guest now. We'll be calling you to side stage in about five or six minutes, so please don't leave this room. Even when we're done with your hair and makeup, please stay here. If you need to use the facilities, do it now because we will be ready for you very soon." She looked at her watch. "I'll be back here in five minutes."

"Sounds great, thank you," Wes said as the producer left the room.

He was so wonderfully calm that I let out a sigh of relief once the door closed behind her.

"I'm so thankful you made it," I said. "I was back here panicking and saying Bible verses to myself, thinking I had to go out there."

"You would've been great," Wes said, trying not to move as the woman put powder on his face. She finished, and he turned to me and smiled. "I cannot believe I made it here with five minutes to spare. Although it might've worked out better if I wouldn't have made it and you had to go out there. You're the one everybody wants to see, anyway."

"That's not true," I said.

The makeup lady glanced at me. She widened her eyes at me and nodded a little as if she agreed with Wes. I could see that she was a fan, and I still wasn't used to that. This was all really recent. The movie trailer Wes made went viral, which directly translated to the success of the movie.

Frank Quinn had helped Wes get a deal with a small streaming service, and for the last three weeks, Full Circle had been their number one movie. It was also going to be featured in three film festivals this year. The unexpected success of this little indie film was what this interview was all about. We were on MTV's Indie Pulse, which was huge.

The movie itself had been an overnight success, and thus, so was I. I was currently in California and had been there for the last week, working out the details about starring in a new limited series based on Neil Britton's Sci-Fi classic, the Red Wall.

As a result of Wes's film, new opportunities had been popping up left and right. Red Wall wasn't my only job prospect on the horizon, and I felt like I had to hold my breath and pray for that same *power, love,* and *sound mind* continually as I navigated these waters.

Wes stayed back in Houston while I was meeting with producers, but he flew out here to meet me for this interview. I knew I would have to do some press surrounding this movie, but a featured segment on MTV was far bigger than anything else I had done, and I needed reinforcements. I had certainly never done anything in front of a studio audience like this.

I was overjoyed when Wes agreed to go on the show in place of me, and my stomach had been in knots when it looked like he wouldn't make it in time. I was going to step up and do it, but I was also relieved now that I didn't have to. Plus, I was just relieved to see Wes in general. One week had felt like a long time.

"You would have been totally fine," Wes said, reaching out for my hand once we were alone in the dressing room.

He stood up, and I stretched upward and gave him a kiss. His mouth was warm and soft, and I missed it so much. It had only been a week, and I was aching for him. My body was alive with anticipation now that I had him by my side. I touched his skin, feeling the hard muscles in his forearms beneath my fingertips.

"I missed you," I said, feeling him.

"I missed you more," he agreed. "I'm really happy about Red Wall, but hated you being gone. How's it going at Jennifer's? That's the one thing I don't ask you on the phone because I never know if she's right there."

Wes knew I was staying with a friend I had made on the set of General Hospital. For the next two nights, before we flew back to Houston, Wes would be staying there as well.

"It's really nice," I said. "She's got her husband and baby and everything, but they have extra bedrooms. I'm on the other side of the house, and I feel comfortable there. You'll be comfortable."

"One minute till I need you, Mr. Quinn, are you ready?" Kat asked the question through the crack in the door.

"I'm ready," Wes answered.

"All right you can come now," she said, opening the door. "You're welcome to wait side stage in the studio, Ms. Morgan, if you want to follow us."

I took her up on that offer and followed them to the studio. I stood behind some partial walls.

I could see Brad, the host, sitting at his desk. I went out far enough to catch a glimpse of a few audience members, but I ducked back quickly, keeping myself hidden. We were only there for a few short minutes before Wes went out.

I watched as Wes spoke to Brad and got settled on the couch. It was a hit talk show and Brad Collins was a cool host. The set was casual, almost set up as if it were a home office. I had seen the television show several times before and it was fascinating to be there, watching Wes sit on that couch.

It all happened really quickly. Before I knew it, the audience was instructed to cheer and then Brad welcomed everyone back to the show and began talking to Wes on camera. I stood quietly and watched from the wings.

"I am here with the red-hot-indie-film director, Wes Quinn."

The audience all cheered, and Brad reacted comically as if it was too loud.

"No, really, Wes is the director of Full Circle the movie, which is everywhere right now. I can't go anywhere online without seeing that picture of Ryder Thorne and Lila Morgan sitting in a train station."

They flashed the picture Brad was talking about, and the audience cheered again, causing Wes to smile, which made my heart pound. I watched him and marveled at the fact that he was just calm and acting like himself.

They spoke about the movie's success since its release. They talked for two minutes or so, a quick easy back-and-forth about the premier. And then my heart jumped when I heard Brad say my name.

"She's amazing," Wes responded.

"I had absolutely no idea that she played the role of her mom in that movie. My wife told me about it the day after we watched it, and I was like, *what?* I had to go look it up. She was so good."

They flashed a photograph of me playing Christine in the movie. I was making a particularly unflattering face in that scene and my special effects makeup was on point. I held in a smile as the audience cheered again when that photo came up.

"I'm sorry to do this, and I don't want to put anyone on the spot, but is Lila Morgan in the house today? I heard a rumor that Lila herself was backstage at our studios today, is she here? Would she possibly want to come out here and talk with us for a minute?"

The audience went off again and Brad looked my way. He was staring past me curiously as if actually wondering whether or not I was in the studio."

"Okay, what do you wanna do, Miss Lila?" Kat said in a point-blank tone. "It's your choice. You can go out there now, or I can tell him you're not here. Choose now."

"I'll go," I said.

I didn't want to do it, but I knew it was the right choice to make. Kat pulled a microphone off of her clipboard and quickly clipped it to my shirt. In the meantime, another PA gave Brad the thumbs up, and he announced that I was in the house and would be right out.

"Just sit on the couch next to Mr. Quinn," she said to me. "Your mic is not hot yet but it will be as soon as you sit down."

"Okay," I agreed, taking a deep breath.

I turned to Brad who waved me over. "Come on out and join us, Miss Lila Morgan!"

The crowd cheered for me as I walked out, and it was honestly surreal. I had been in curtain calls where audiences cheered, but that felt more collective. This time, they were cheering for me.

I grounded myself by repeating the *power, love, sound mind,* phrase as I somehow put one foot in front of the other and found my way over to Wes on that couch. I shook Brad's hand on my way over and then I had a seat, taking in my surroundings, and remembering to breathe and smile.

The audience had been cheering the whole time I went out there and I continued to smile, thanking them with humble nods as it began to quiet down.

Chapter 17

Brad Collins stared at the camera, shaking his head with a big smile. "What a special treat we have here. The lovely Lila Morgan, right here in our studio today." He tapped the index cards on the desk. "Listen, if you have not seen the Full Circle movie, and I think there are only a few people in the world who haven't seen it. You do not know what you're missing. It really is a treat. Visually, it's a treat. Did you direct the cinematography, Wes?"

"I did," Wes said humbly.

Brad gestured at me. "And those two, Anna and Ben, they just connected. It was fun to watch, and I'm not even the romantic type."

"It wasn't a romance," Wes said seriously.

I smiled at that. He was jealous. I was sitting on the couch with my real-life prince charming, and my mind wandered. I had to catch up and realize that he was talking about the movie. We were on a talk show to discuss the movie. These types of thoughts went through my head between sentences.

"Ryder is a good friend of mine, and he did an outstanding job."

"He did. But this young woman is the star, I have to say." The audience cheered. "Unbelievable, that Christine character."

"That was all Lila. That was her inspiration. She's the best."

"Now, I don't mean to put either of you on the spot. But I just have to know… I have to ask… there have been a few couple-looking photos of you two surfacing…" He trailed off, and the production crew flashed a photograph of Wes and me. I turned to look at the screen.

It was us holding hands at the premiere, and then they flashed another one of us holding hands on the sidewalk. The second one was from the other day, right before I had left Houston, and it was one I hadn't seen of us. I glanced at Wes with a confused expression, wondering if we were famous enough to be photographed in public now.

"She's looking confused. Uh-oh, I didn't mean to bring it up if it's not a thing." Brad tossed his stack of notecards onto the desk as if he had really messed up.

"No, it's a thing," I said, nodding and assuring Brad. "I was just wondering who took that picture of us."

"Oh, this? Where'd we get this picture? Our production team is on the ball with this kind of thing."

"Google!" someone yelled out from backstage.

"After some intense investigation, we found it on Google," Brad said, causing the audience to laugh. "A good-old Google search."

"Wow," I said, feeling stunned at the sight of my first paparazzi photo.

"So, you said it's a thing, Lila? Is there a thing between you two?"

Both of us reached out for each other's hands when he asked that. "Yes," Wes said in an easy, matter-of-fact tone.

"Would you describe Lila Morgan as your girlfriend?" Brad asked, looking at Wes and seeming serious.

Wes glanced at me. He was dressed sharply for the interview. He had been on a flight and then stuck in traffic and he looked fresh and more handsome than ever. "Yes, I'd say she's my girlfriend," he said, clarifying cautiously and causing the audience to laugh and applaud.

"How about you, Lila?" Brad said. "Did you know that, or is this news to you?"

"Oh, I knew. Wes and I go way back. We met when we were kids, just like the movie."

I trailed off glancing guiltily at Wes and knowing I had mentioned unscripted things.

"Whoa, whoa, whoa, wait a minute," Brad said, looking confused. "What?"

"She's right," Wes agreed.

"That's a picture of us you don't have. There's a photograph of Wes and me together when we were babies. Meeting Wes was one of my earliest memories."

"Wait," Brad said, looking and sounding confused and causing the audience to laugh. "Have you known each other your *whole lives*?"

"No. We just met last year when he hired me to do the movie," I said. "We didn't find out we had met as babies until we were already, you know, dating. My mom found a picture of us."

"Yeah, and my parents had no idea we had met," Wes said. "They had never seen that picture of me or even knew I interacted with Lila or her family."

"That is unbelievable," Brad said.

"It really is," Wes said. "I thought I got the movie inspiration from seeing a live birth, but maybe it was bigger than that. Maybe I was just supposed to write it so I could find Lila again."

The audience cheered at that even though Wes wasn't trying to get that response.

"So, is it safe to say that you'll be working together again?"

"Professionally?" Wes said. "Never mind, it doesn't matter. The answer is yes. We'll be working together again for sure."

Our hands were still casually interlocked on Wes's leg.

"I would love to work with Wes again, professionally… and any other way he… wants to work… with me…" I spoke in a happy but choppy tone, and it drew a round of laughter from the audience.

Wes laughed and pulled me in with an arm around my shoulder. I loved him, and I glanced at him with an expression that said as much.

"Lila's got other jobs in the works right now, but we like each other a lot, both professionally and… personally."

"Oh, my goodness, you have no idea how much I wish we had more time to talk to the two of you, but I have to get down to business, here, and play a clip of this movie."

The producers played a clip of the moment when Ben realized he had been at Anna's birth.

I had obsessed about this movie. I starred in it, then I helped Wes with the editing process. I had seen this clip so many times that I felt like I was living in the Matrix as I watched it—like it was moving in slow motion because of how familiar it was to me.

I thought about everything while it was playing. I thought about the audience and the fact that Wes was still holding my hand in front of all of them.

"We were going to play a clip of you playing Christine, but I guess after you told that story, our producers found the other part of that movie. I wish we had that picture of the two of you when you were babies. That would complete this story."

"I have it on my phone," I said.

"She has it on her phone," Brad said, sounding comically stunned again and staring at the audience.

I was not expecting to go on stage and therefore I had my phone in the back pocket of my jeans. I took it out and set my phone on my leg, quickly scrolling through my personal photographs and trying to find the photograph. I was relatively sure this was not the right thing to do on a talk show interview, but I found it difficult to do anything but be myself.

It took me a few seconds, but I found the photograph and then I instantly stood up and leaned over so that I could hand my whole phone to Brad who eagerly took it from me.

"Well... good... grief," he said slowly as he stared at the screen.

He turned the phone around and rested it securely on the desk so that the cameraman could zoom in on it.

I smiled as the audience reacted with a collective, "Awwww."

"Is that you with the bandages all over you?" he asked Wes.

"Yes," Wes answered.

"Did you remember this happening?"

"No, I didn't, actually."

"It's one of my very first memories, and I'm eighteen months older than him.

Brad raised his eyebrows at Wes as if he liked the idea of an older woman, and the audience laughed again. "Listen, you two... I'm so sorry we have to say goodnight. This has been a special treat having both of you here. I wish you both all the happiness in the world. I really do. Full Circle is a work of art, and you can check it out on Tristar Plus. Thanks again to both of you for being here. Let's give it up for Wes Quinn and Lila Morgan!"

The audience cheered, and the producers gestured for them to do it even louder. They cued indie rock, which was loud and played while they took a commercial.

Some of the PAs spoke to the audience, but we turned our attention to Brad.

"Thank you, guys, for being here," Brad said to us again.

He handed the stack of cards to the producer. She came to stand in front of us with her back to the audience. "I don't mean to rush you off, but you might want to head out right behind the curtain, there, if you don't want people to start trying to get your attention. You'll want to head to the backstage area to avoid the hassle."

I was new enough to all this that I didn't see talking to fans as a hassle, but I figured they wanted us to go quietly without causing a scene, so Wes and I stood up and took off toward backstage. Someone yelled my name—a woman. I turned and several people waved at me. I waved back in that general direction since I wasn't sure who said it.

"I love youuu, Lila!" someone else said—a man. I smiled and blew a kiss in that general direction and gave a wave before turning to follow Kat off stage.

It only took a few minutes for us to wrap up at the studio and make our way to the car I had rented at the airport a week earlier. Wes had a driver drop him off at the studio, and he brought a bag with him which we stashed in the trunk. Wes drove, and we plugged in directions to Jennifer's house. My rental was a discreet grey Audi. It had tinted windows, and so far, I had no trouble going around town in it. That paparazzi photo Brad showed was a surprise to me.

"Did you really not know about those photos of us?" Wes asked from over the console.

"I was seriously just thinking about that," I said to him. "I've been living in a bubble at Jennifer's for the last week. I didn't know that picture existed. I haven't seen it."

Wes reached over the console, and I held his hand. "I didn't know Brad was going to bring it up. I didn't know he was going to do any of that. Are you okay?"

"How do you think it went?" I asked.

"I think you did great and it went great… great job. But I also think I almost had to fight some dude who yelled out that he loved you right there in front of me. What was that?" He made a comically stunned face, and I laughed.

"I thought it was sweet," I said.

"Sweet?" Wes asked, furrowing his eyebrows. I knew he was just messing around, but I loved it. "Only one guy gets to love you," he said, being lightheartedly stubborn.

"More importantly, I only love one guy," I said.

"That is more important," he said.

I held onto his hand tenderly, embracing it because I missed him that much.

"Are you hungry?" he asked.

"Yes. I didn't realize it, but yes, I am. I need to eat. I haven't eaten much today."

"What kind of food?"

"Let me take you to a place," I said.

Chapter 18

I reprogramed the GPS to take us to a restaurant I had found months before when I was living out here. I knew I wanted to take Wes there some time, and this seemed like a good moment to make that happen.

"It's a garden," I said. "I think of it as a garden first. The restaurant is just a way to go over there and experience the yard and the garden, really. There are plants everywhere, Wes—it's gorgeous. It's a small mom-and-pop place."

"Do you think they'll have a table?"

"It'll barely be six o'clock when we get there, so hopefully."

"What kind of food?"

"Farm to table."

"I could have guessed that by what you've already said."

"I think I had roasted Cornish game hen last time. They always have a lot of veggies and stuff like that. Weird stuff, too. I had a dandelion salad last time."

"Lion's teeth. I've had that."

"What?"

"You said dandelion, and that's what it means."

"Lions teeth?"

"Yeah, or tooth of the lion, or something having to do with lion and tooth. It's French, dent, like dentist or tooth, dent-de-lion, tooth-of-lion. Or something like that. It's because of the jagged leaf."

"I'm not surprised you've had dandelion. You've eaten everything known to man." It was the truth. Wes had traveled the world and had eaten things like squid ink soup and roasted crickets. "Are you going to eat dandelions tonight?" I added.

"Probably not, honestly." He touched his own stomach. "Unless it's an appetizer. I'm too hungry for a salad. I'll probably eat one or two of those game hens you were talking about."

It took us fifteen minutes to get to The Green House, and the small parking lot was already full when we got there. It was in an older house, and we parked in the lot next to it. Some of the seating was inside in different rooms of the house, but the best seating was outside, in the backyard, on their covered patio. It was a jungle back there and it made you feel like you had left the city. I couldn't wait to show Wes.

"You're going to love it," I said to him after we parked. "Maybe, if we have to wait, we can go next door and get ice cream to hold us over until dinner. We could eat dessert first."

"Let's just go in and see how long the wait is, and then we can decide," he said.

We were greeted at the door by two people—a male and female—standing at a host station.

"Hello, thank you for joining us this evening. do you have a reservation?"

"Uh, no, the last time I came was with a friend, and we, I don't think you were this busy."

I got lost in thought thinking about my last experience there. I had been with two friends from General Hospital, so I was starting to think that was why we had gotten a table so easily.

"My friend might have had reservations that day. How long is the wait?"

"The patio is reservation only, and I'm afraid we're booked. I can get you a table in the house in forty-five minutes to an hour."

I glanced at Wes with a hesitant face. "I think the main reason I wanted to come was for the patio, anyway," I spoke discreetly, but I knew they didn't care.

"I'm sorry, excuse me, but are you, did you star in that movie in the train station?"

I looked at the male host, since he was the one who had asked. "I did star in that," I said.

"Hold on, please I need to…" he trailed off and leaned in to whisper in the woman's ear.

I looked at Wes with an innocent shrug.

"We have a special table. We need to clear it and have it ready to use again in an hour, but if you can choose your menu items quickly, we have a table that can accommodate you right now."

"We can eat quickly," Wes said.

The female host took off, and we followed her into the house. I thought we were going to get seated out onto the patio, but the host took a turn and went through the house in a different direction. I felt bummed that we wouldn't be able to see the garden, but I was hungry and I knew Wes was, too.

"This is a private exit," she said, pointing at a door at the end of the hall. "When you're finished eating you can leave through this door."

She reached out and opened a velvet rope that was hanging across a staircase. It had a sign that said employees only, and she smiled and gestured for us to go up. Wes led the way and we went upstairs. There was a hallway with multiple doors, and we saw an employee coming out of one of the doors, carrying an empty tray. He nodded at us and let us pass, keeping his head down in the most professional way possible.

"We're heading to the owner's table," she said, coming up from behind us to lead the way. "It's reserved for special guests." She looked at me and smiled like she was nervous and excited to have me eat at the restaurant, which was still foreign to me. Wes squeezed my hand discreetly, and I smiled at him.

We walked through a door and onto a gorgeous outdoor patio. It was the upstairs balcony. It was everything the garden below was, only it was smaller and more private. It was just about the most beautiful place I had ever seen. There were lion fountains on the walls, spitting water into a trough that wrapped around the balcony. Everything was ornate and gorgeous. It was a miniature version of the downstairs garden, only better. There were lush, beautiful flowering plants all around us in spite of it being February.

"You can view the downstairs patio through the vines over here." She pointed to our left, and I looked toward the place she was indicating before glancing all around. There was a small table for two in the center of this unbelievable private patio.

"I do not want to rush you, but we can't budge on reservations for this room, I hope you understand."

"I understand," I said. "Thank you. This is beautiful. We'll decide what we want to eat quickly."

"Would you like to look at the menu now?" she asked. "I could stay here and take your order. Everything is made fresh, so it takes our chef a little longer."

"I am happy to order now," I said. I held out my hand for the menu even though we hadn't even sat in a chair yet.

"Oh, I'm sorry. You can go ahead and have a seat. I don't mean to rush you that much."

"You're not. I'm just taking in the scenery," I said. I maneuvered casually to the table in the center of the patio. "I really appreciate you letting us eat out here. It's gorgeous."

"It's the most beautiful place I know," she agreed, handing me a menu. "And I get to be here every day. I know you'll enjoy it out here."

We took a minute to look over the menu.

Wes ordered a sirloin, and I ordered baked chicken with orzo. The host recommended a few veggies and a dessert, and we easily and quickly decided on several options which all sounded amazing.

"Just a little about your balcony before I head downstairs. The owner spends a lot of time in the kitchen, and his wife comes up here. She's the one who has made this patio what it is. It is constant work—pruning, planting, and fertilizing. We have a full-time gardener on staff for the patio downstairs, but the owner's wife handles this area by herself. She asks politely that you don't cut any of her flowers. Please leave them here for others to enjoy."

Someone else came outside, and we all looked her way. "Laney will take your drink orders and be serving you for the remainder of your time here. There's a switch on the table. Simply flip it if you'd like to call for service."

Laney, indeed, stuck around and took our drink order, and within another minute or two, Wes and I were alone on the balcony.

"What just happened?" I whispered with wide eyes.

"You're famous, that's what happened."

"Seriously?"

"Yes. They recognized you, and here we are, at the owner's table."

"This is un-believable." I said, looking around. "How beautiful can you get? I feel like I'm in Tuscany. Is this what Tuscany's like?" I asked.

He leaned back in his chair and stared at me. "This is way better than Tuscany."

"You haven't even gone over there and looked down."

"I know, but this is already better than anything I saw in Tuscany," he said, staring at me. Wes was dark and mysterious, and I needed to get closer to him. I leaned over and reached for his hand.

"Come on," I said. "Let's go look over the rail.

The balcony was on a corner of the house, so we were surrounded on two sides by building and on two sides by railing. There was a tree and some vines, and it felt private up there, even when we stood at the edge and looked over.

"These are crazy-looking plants," I said, touching the giant leaves of the largest elephant ears I had ever seen. "It's basically a tree," I added, looking at it. "Do you think it's okay for me to touch it?" I asked, pulling my hand away and looking back at Wes.

He grinned at me and pulled me into his arms. I went easily, snuggling close to him. I loved being near him, and I breathed, smiling at the comfort I felt in that moment. I was safe and surrounded by luxury and love. I felt rich. My acting work technically hadn't translated into money yet, but that would be coming soon.

I was working out the contract for Red Wall, and if all went as planned, I could be making half a million dollars for twelve episodes over two seasons. My character would be Blanche. She was a principal side character who made appearances in most episodes of the show.

I hadn't made any money for playing Blanche yet, and none of my other prospects had come to fruition, but I still felt like the richest woman in the whole world. That balcony did it to me. It was lush beauty like I had rarely seen. The lion fountains really put it over the top. Wes held me securely, and my mind drifted to random good thoughts as I stood there in his arms.

"It felt weird to me, saying you were my girlfriend to Brad Collins," he said.

I pulled back to look at Wes with a worried expression. "Why?"

"You know why. Girlfriend seems so… it doesn't seem like enough to call you that."

"Oh, not enough? Good."

"What did you think I meant?" he asked.

"You know, I thought you might have been embarrassed that he brought it up on TV."

"No. Opposite. I felt weird *only* calling you my girlfriend."

"That felt weird to me, too," I said, getting closer to him, flirting with him. "I felt terrible saying that."

He laughed a little. "I'm being serious."

"I'm being serious, too," I said. "I want you to call me whatever you want to call me."

"My wife," he said.

"Yes," I agreed with no hesitation.

"Don't agree so easily," he said. "I'm going to take you up on it and start calling you that."

I shrugged. "Okay, but to call me that, I have to be it."

"You have to be my wife?"

I nodded. It was still February, which meant the sun went down early. It was now dark enough that the automatic lights came on. There were string lights on our balcony and we could also see lights down below in the garden. They all came on at the same time, and I felt like I was in a fairytale. I didn't mention it, but I did notice that the lights had come on when I agreed to become his wife.

"A lot of planning goes into me being able to call you that, I think. We have to go through a bunch of steps, like a ring and a proposal."

"Or, you could just ask me now, and we could elope today or tomorrow."

"Marry meeeee," he said in a groaning tone.

I giggled because Wes slunk down as if he was melting. He held onto me, hugging me, from his new, crouched-down position. It took me a second to realize that he had gone all the way to a knee.

"I'm asking you to please marry me."

I smiled and pulled on his hand, causing him to stand again. I went to him, holding him, getting my body as close to him as it could get.

"Yes," I said, holding onto him. "I will definitely marry you, Wes. I would love to marry you. I don't need anything elaborate."

He pulled back, staring down at me. Our faces were only a few inches apart. His expression made me concerned because he seemed serious and almost worried.

"We can't do it like this, though," he said. "We have to have a ring and a proposal and stuff—an engagement."

"No, we really don't," I said. "Unless you need it. I am ready for everything with you. I have no doubts, fears, or preconceived notions about what an engagement should look like. I would seriously go to Las Vegas with you tomorrow. Tonight."

Wes cleared his throat and took a deep breath. "You should be the levelheaded one here," he warned. "If you look at the two of us on paper, I am the wild one who would do something crazy like run off to Vegas and marry his girlfriend. You're the calm one who dates someone for a long time before a normal proposal and a normal marriage."

"Are you calling me boring?" I asked. "Is this a dare? Because I was the one who was thinking about Vegas in the first place."

"Lila Jane Morgan."

"Yes?"

"Don't tempt me. I already warned you that I'm the wild one." He pressed himself against me, kissing me with an open mouth for a few short glorious seconds just to prove his point. I let him. I opened my mouth, kissing him back, holding him against me, feeling desperate to become his wife—to do wife things with him.

He continued, covering me with his kiss as if he could read my mind.

"Pleeease," I said begging in a whisper when he finally broke the kiss.

"I'm warning you, I will agree to this and drive across the state line if you keep pushing it."

"I'm warning you, Wes, that I want it to happen, so I'm likely to keep pushing until it does."

"People would find out," he said.

I shrugged. "We've been together. It's not like we met yesterday. Plus, it's our business, not theirs. It's our lives."

"Don't you feel like you deserve better than a Vegas wedding?" he asked.

"Ask yourself that," I said. "You would be half of this wedding. Do you think *you* deserve better than a Vegas wedding? It seems like you're doubting it."

"No. Just, no, Lila. If it was up to me, I would've run off to Vegas and married you months ago."

"Well, why didn't you?" I asked. I scrunched my face up a little, which caused him to smile and take me into his arms.

Chapter 19

Wes Quinn

The server came onto the balcony with drinks and an amuse-bouche. Wes and Lila split apart just a bit, but they stayed standing near each other at the edge of the balcony. Laney set the drinks and small plates on the table. They thanked her, and she said she'd be back soon with the rest of the food.

"I wonder what it is," Lila said, squinting at the table.

"Let's check it out," Wes said, pulling her over there.

"They're different. Which one do you want? Do you think they meant for us to have a certain one?"

"What do you mean?" Wes asked, sitting down and looking at the food.

"Well, she put this one where my bag was. Do you think that means it's meant for me?"

"I don't think the chef would be that specific, do you?"

"I don't know. I don't know how these things work I've never been given an amuse-bouche before."

"Did they not give you one the last time you came to this restaurant?"

"No," she said inspecting it.

Hers was a small purple circle that looked to be about the consistency of stiff mashed potatoes. It had a crust on the bottom and was topped with a little bit of cream and some herbs. Wes loved watching her look at it.

"You can have mine too, if you want," he said, pushing his plate over to her since she seemed so entertained. His was equally as delicate and pretty, but different. Wes's looked like it would be savory with a hashbrown-like crust, but it was about the shape of a miniature Reese's cup.

"Why aren't you eating it?" she asked, looking concerned.

"I will, but I want you to have it, if you want it."

"No, I'm just excited to try mine. I have no idea what this is. It looks like a mystery patty."

"It is a mystery patty," he said, laughing.

"It's purple. I don't know if it's salty or sweet."

"You won't know until it's in your mouth."

Her eyes widened. "I might not even know then." She smiled as she reached in for it and then popped it into her mouth. Her eyes got wider and she grinned with her mouth closed and full. She looked like an adorable chipmunk, and Wes desperately wanted to marry her. He wanted her to be the mother of his children. He wanted her to smile at them with that full-cheeked chipmunk smile.

He was tempted to bring up Vegas again. Wes watched her chew and swallow her food, and he realized he was no better than the guy who had just yelled out to her in the studio. He was a smitten fan just like the rest of them. Her willingness to play Christine brought the movie to its fullest potential and busted the hinges off of Lila's doors of success. The funny thing was that she had only done it to help him out.

His chest ached and the word *Veeegaaas* was again on the tip of his tongue. He kept quiet. He knew she deserved a ring and a proposal, and he wasn't going to rush things for his own desires. But she was smiling as she finished the bite, and he got caught looking at her face again. He felt needy and selfish, and he reluctantly peeled his eyes off of her and focused on his own food.

"Are you sure you don't want it?" he asked before he ate it.

"Yes, I'm sure. I want you to have it."

Wes reached out and put the bite of food into his mouth.

"What do you think?" she asked as he chewed.

"Tastes a little like breakfast," he said.

"Mine didn't taste like breakfast at all," she said. "Mine tasted like garlic and butter and… dirt."

"Dirt?" he asked, making a face that caused her to laugh.

"Dirt in a good way," she clarified. "…like maybe some root vegetable or something. It was really good. It tasted natural."

"I'm glad I got mine," he said, side-eyeing her description.

"It was good," she assured him. "It just had an earthy quality to it. It was interesting. If I had another one, I would want you to try it. We should have eaten half of each other's so we could taste both of them."

"I knew you wanted mine," he said. "You should have taken it when I offered."

She laughed because he was being lighthearted, teasing her. "I didn't want yours, but we should have thought about sharing. Mine was interesting enough that I regret you not being able to try it."

"I think that's the whole point of those things, though," he said. "I think you're supposed to take them in one bite."

She regarded Wes. She wore a half-smile, and she stared unrepentantly at him from across the table for what must have been ten or fifteen seconds.

"What are you thinking about?" he asked.

"I missed you so much. My heart is beating fast just looking at you. I want to come over there to you."

"What's stopping you?" he asked.

She got up out of her chair and walked over to Wes, and he felt like he was in a dream. She came to him, sitting carefully on his leg. He pulled her closer, forcing her off-balance and causing her to put more weight on him. She let out a little squeal and wiggled as if she was trying to not be heavy.

"Come here, you're not hurting me," he said, pulling her in. She rested against him, letting him hold onto her as he leaned back in his chair. He breathed a long sigh as they got settled, and it caused her to do the same.

"I'm so happy you're here," she said. "Thank you for coming and doing that show."

"You were the star of that show, I didn't do anything," he replied.

"Yes, you did. I could've never been that comfortable without you."

"Thank you, but you would do fine. I don't think you quite grasp how much star quality you have."

"Thank you for saying that, but it has nothing to do with being a star. I rely on study and practice. I don't know how far that'll get me."

"To the very top," he said. "It'll get you as far as you want to go. You're already there."

He held her close to him, absentmindedly stroking her shoulder with his hand. Then suddenly, she jumped out of his hands like she had been struck by lightning. Wes didn't even hear the door or see it open, but Lila did, and she jumped off of his lap and made her way discreetly to the other side of the table.

The server came in, and the two of them talked to her from their positions across the table. She gave them an update on their order and told them a bit about the balcony and a few of the special plants that were growing there. They thanked her, and she left with their empty plates in her hand.

Wes looked at her with a sly smile. "You didn't have to get up when she came in here."

"Yes, I did," she said. "That wouldn't look good if she caught us like that."

"What do you mean?"

"I mean, I wouldn't want a picture of us to surface like that, so I figured we shouldn't get caught."

"Why don't you want us to be photographed together? Was it that photograph Brad had today?"

"No, I don't care if we get photographed together. I like us getting photographed together. I'm not saying that. I just know that my parents wouldn't approve of any kind of..." she hesitated. "...lap-sitting photographs. You know, before marriage."

"Ah, yes, the old *no public-lap-sitting photos before marriage* rule. I forgot about that one."

She squinted at him and he grinned innocently. "Marry me, then," she said. "And I won't care what kind of photographs get taken of us."

"Lila Morgan, you're daring me a lot tonight. There's only so much a man can take."

"What does that mean?" she asked.

"It means you're going to cause me to drag you to Las Vegas."

"You would not be dragging me, Wes. I'm trying to be a proper lady here, and I'm trying to let you do the asking, but I've been sitting over here dying for you to bring it up again."

"Bring what up? Going to Vegas?"

"Yes. Running away and getting married."

"How can the same woman who just jumped off my lap when someone came in also say you would be willing to do that?"

"Those are two different things. I wouldn't be jumping off of your lap if we were married."

Wes stared at her from across the table with an expression that said he was trying to be patient and find the right words.

"Let me try to make sure we're clear," he said. "The shenanigans we are talking about would affect a lot of things. There would be no normal proposal, no inviting friends to a wedding, no invitations, no showers, and bachelorette parties and all the stuff that happens with a wedding. I wouldn't want to get married in Vegas and then go back to Houston and do all of that stuff. So, if you want those things, we can just wait a few days or weeks. I can get you a ring, and we can decide what we're doing. We can start planning now, if you want."

"What do you think I want?" she asked.

She took a sip of her water and looked at him. Both of them were speaking in a calm relaxed tone, neither of them in a hurry to go anywhere.

"You need to tell me that," he said. "Because I'm up for whatever."

"Really? You don't seem like it. It seems like you're the one who's trying to talk me out of it."

"Out of what?" he asked. "Going to Vegas?"

"Yes. You keep telling me I don't want to do it."

"Because I don't want you to do something you'd regret. Girls like taking pictures of their wedding and stuff. They like to invite friends over and plan a bunch of parties and things like that. And then, once it's done, then we're married. We're stuck together like glue."

"Well, being stuck to you doesn't seem like a bad thing, Wes. And do you really think I need all that? You know me."

"I know, but I don't know about that stuff. We've never talked about a wedding."

"Our lives have been a whirlwind since we met."

"What do you want? Do you not care about the white dress and the party and all that? Because it doesn't matter at all to me. I want to do what you want to do."

"I would have already married you by now if it was up to me," she said, still speaking in a calm, unhurried tone. "I know you have a big family and you're an only child, so I figured your mom would want you to have a big-deal wedding. I thought it would be forever for you to propose and marry me because of how your mom would want to do it."

"What does my mom have to do with us getting married?" Wes asked.

She opened her mouth like she was about to say something and then she closed it again. "Let's sit here and think about it for a second," she said taking a deep breath.

They were separated by eight or ten feet of space and a table, and yet her eyes connected them. They sat like that for a minute or two, surrounded by the sounds of the fountains and low music and murmur from below.

"I want to do it," she said, finally.

"What exactly do you want to do?"

"I want to marry you as soon as possible. Today. Whenever."

"There's a chance it'll make it to the press," he said.

"I know."

"Are you sure you're going to… are you going to be okay with it in the long run? Being married? Are you sure you're not just getting swept up in the moment?"

"What moment?" she asked.

"Not seeing me for a week," he said. "The television show and everything."

"I'm not swept up in anything, Wes. I knew weeks ago that I was going to marry you the minute you asked me."

"What about your parents?" he asked.

"I'll tell them after we do it," she said.

They were speaking in comically calm, slow tones for the intensity of the subject matter.

"What about *your* parents?" she asked.

"Same," he returned. "I'll just tell them after we do it."

Chapter 20

Lila Morgan

The server came back with our food just as we decided that we were going to Vegas to get married. I had been in some surreal scenarios in my life, some with Wes, but this afternoon and evening were extremely surreal. My mind was swimming—but my heart was full. I had the feeling that our elopement was actually going to happen.

"Tonight?" I asked, continuing our conversation casually as our server came toward the table.

"Yes, tonight," Wes answered confidently.

I shrugged. "I'm free right after this, if you want."

"Okay, sure, that'll work for me," Wes said in a friendly, business-like tone.

I turned to smile at our server who had approached us with a tray of food. She set my food in front of me and then did the same for Wes. I stared at it, feeling like I could barely appreciate how upscale and wonderful it was. I wasn't hungry at all. I was too in love for basic things like eating food.

I couldn't help but think about how much my life was about to change. I was completely serious about eloping, and I knew Wes was also. It was going to happen. He had been staring at me, but then he turned to respond to the server.

It was a good thing Wes knew what to say to her. I had to concentrate on remembering to breathe. He sat up in his chair, glancing at the food and remarking about it to Laney, our server. She laughed and responded back to him. He was dripping with masculine energy, and I loved watching him talk to people.

I had a massive crush on Wes Quinn, and there was no way I was going to pass up the chance to marry him. If he was willing to go to Vegas, we were going to Vegas. I was filled with so much excitement that I could hardly sit still or even take in my surroundings.

"Did you hear?" he said to me.

"Hear what?" I asked.

"You were right about the amuse-bouche. She said it was purple potato."

"Oh, that's cool," I said, nodding. "Thank you so much, this looks delicious."

I stared at my food. Laney explained a couple of things about our selections, where the produce was grown, and how it was cooked. But my mind wandered, and I only half-listened to her, nodding and smiling at what I thought were the appropriate times.

The door was open and another server came onto the patio rolling a complicated-looking cart. The two

of them stood to the side and talked about some sort
of flambé procedure that the chef would do later.

I assumed they would leave soon, but I didn't
really care. I watched as Wes leaned toward me,
looking at my food. "Everything looks really good,"
he said.

"I'm glad you're hungry," I said, widening my
eyes at him.

He grinned at me, understanding what I was
saying. "Just eat a few bites and I'll eat mine and
then finish yours."

They were small portions, so I wasn't surprised
to hear him say that. I nodded and took a small bite
of pasta, which was delicious and flavorful. It had a
particular taste to it, and I assumed it was truffle oil
even though I wasn't sure.

"I'm having really good ideas," he said.

"I'm having good ideas too," I agreed dazedly,
causing him to laugh.

"No, seriously. I have a plan."

"What?"

"Let's leave here, go to Vegas. We can stay the
night there, and then instead of coming back here or
going back to Houston, let's go to the lake house.
Let's leave Vegas and go straight to Arkansas. We
can fly, or we could just take off driving across the
country if you want. We could be there for a few
days, maybe a week—a makeshift honeymoon. Your
uncle said it's empty a lot in the winter. We could
theoretically go anywhere you want, I just figured it

185

was available and I knew we could probably get some privacy over there—fly under the radar."

"It's an amazing idea, Wes. I can go back to Jennifer's to get my stuff after we eat." We took a minute to eat a few bites, and then I continued speaking casually. "While we're on the way to Vegas, we can talk about whether or not we want to drive or fly, but Arkansas sounds amazing. I need to ask my uncle if it's… there's actually a calendar. I can get to it on my phone. I'll do that in a minute. The lake house is a great idea, though."

Wes looked a little stunned that I had agreed to everything so casually, but our server approached the table again so I got quiet. "We'll give you a few minutes to finish your meal, and then the chef will be up to finish your dessert. Is there anything else I can get you while you eat?"

"This is great," Wes said. "Do you need anything?" he added, looking at me.

"No, thank you," I said, trying not to seem in a hurry.

"It's great, thank you," Wes said.

We sat there for a moment, tasting our food and each others. Wes was still thinking, looking introspective.

"Why do you seem quiet?" I asked.

"I'm not. I'm thinking about possible scenarios. You're just agreeing to everything so easily, and I want you to know that I'll wait, and I'll take you anywhere you want to go."

"Honestly, Wes, I want to drive away from this restaurant, pick up my stuff, and go to the quickest chapel we can find. If there was one at this house, I would do it right this second. But I think Vegas is our best bet. I don't even care if it's Elvis Presley, honestly. I say we pick the quickest place. Can it happen tonight? We could spend the night in Vegas and then just take off driving to Arkansas, like you said. We have maps, and we can stop at stores if we need anything. Let's head to the lake house. I can do research from the road. Maybe we can stop and tour a cave or something. Why do you look so serious? Do you not like caves?"

"No, Lila, I'm just trying to remind you that… I need to remind you that, in our relationship, you're the more conservative one. You're the one who talks me out of making quick major life decisions."

"Are you saying you don't want to marry me? Are you having second thoughts?"

He closed his eyes, making a serious, dramatic expression. His face was perfect. I stared at his mouth.

"Absolutely not," he said. "I'm just warning you, Lila, that you sound convinced when you're saying all of this. You sound like you really want to do it. If you continue to bring it up, I am going to marry you today and not feel bad about it."

"Please don't feel bad about it," I said. "I say we get on the road, the quicker the better."

Wes set down his fork and looked at me in such a way that let me know something was about to happen. His chair screeched as he scooted back, and then he stared at me, hesitating for all of two seconds before he stood up abruptly.

"Let's go," he said.

"Now?" I asked, smiling uncontrollably. I set down my own fork before he ever answered. He gave me a nod and held out a hand, and I stood. I placed my hand in his from over the table, and he took off, pulling me along.

Out the door and down the hallway we went, walking so quickly that I couldn't help but laugh a little. I wiped the grin off of my face when we ran into our server at the top of the stairway. "Is everything all right?" she asked, regarding us with a cautious, serious expression.

"It was wonderful," he said. "We ate most of it, but we're going to have to miss the dessert." As he was speaking, Wes let go of my hand long enough to reach into his pocket. I watched him take out his wallet and hand her some money. It all happened quickly, but I knew there was a hundred-dollar bill on top and there were multiple bills. I didn't care how much it was. The server looked happy as she took them from him, but then her face turned regretful when Wes moved as if we were about to leave.

"I'm sorry you didn't get to meet Chef Daniel."

"I'm sorry too," Wes said. "Please tell him how much we loved the food. It really was a great experience here. We'll definitely be back the next time we're in town."

She stared at us as Wes stopped speaking, and I could tell she hated that we were leaving. It wasn't regret for the restaurant's sake, she was regretful for her own. She was starstruck which was still unbelievable to me. But I didn't have time to take it all in because Wes took my hand and headed off down the stairs.

"Thanks again!" he called.

And then we were on the move.

We walked through the restaurant and then outside before we found the car in the parking lot.

Wes had all of his things in a large duffel bag, and I considered leaving for Vegas right then since Jennifer's house was thirty minutes away. We ended up going back there to get my things, but we were quick about it and only talked to my friend and her husband for a few minutes before getting on the road.

It would be late by the time we made it to Vegas. We started off with every intention of finding the quickest place and getting married that night. But during the trip, we talked about it and decided to wait until the following day.

Wes drove while I made all sorts of reservations—two rooms for tonight, a wedding ceremony the following day, and one room for the following evening.

We could have rushed it and gotten married anytime we wanted—right when we arrived, or in the middle of the night. But I was able to find a pretty little chapel with great reviews, and I made a reservation for 1:15 the following afternoon.

We decided to stay at the Bellagio. Wes's grandfather had connections there years ago, and Wes had stayed there before, so he recommended it. He said I could mention his grandfather's name, but I decided to call and reserve rooms without trying to do any of that. Wes agreed, and I made a reservation under his name so that we had rooms waiting for us when we pulled up.

It was almost midnight when we arrived at the hotel, and it was still busy in there. I had never been to Vegas. I had seen some beautiful buildings and architecture, but these Vegas hotels and casinos were on another level. I felt like I was in a movie as I walked into the main entrance. Even with all of the grandeur, though, the main thing on my mind was Wes.

He took care of our valet and luggage, and then we walked to the main desk. Wes walked ahead of me, pulling me along, holding my hand. I glanced at him, feeling all worked up inside that I was about to be his wife. I had already imagined things that would happen with us, and seeing him, seeing the backside

of his body move in his nice, well-fitting clothing…
my thoughts became distracting.

I peeled my eyes off of him and noticed that the woman at the desk stared at me with an intense expression as we approached.

Wes squeezed my hand and turned to me. "I think she recognizes you," he said, discreetly.

"From where?" I asked, not remembering, in that moment, that I was a famous actress now.

"From the movie," Wes said, barely moving his mouth as we walked.

"Good evening, I'm Gwen, will you be staying with us tonight? It would be a pleasure to have you with us."

"I, uh, made the reservation under Quinn. Wesley Quinn," I said.

She smiled and typed his name into the computer. "Yes, for two rooms?" she asked. She glanced behind us briefly. "I really enjoyed your movie," she added, hopefully.

"Thank you," I said.

Wes said the same phrase at the same time, and she looked at him with a curious expression. She was a professional, and she kept her facial reactions to a minimum, but I could tell she wanted to know more about us.

"Were you in the same movie?" she asked.

"I directed it."

Her eyes widened. "Full Circle?"

"Yes," he said.

"Oh, my. I really enjoyed that movie. You both did a great job. Okay, we have your rooms under Quinn." She stared at the screen. "They're down as… hold on, if you will. I'd like to talk to my manager about getting an upgrade for you." She spoke quietly since there were others around.

"We don't mind," I said.

We got our upgrade.

Then we went to our own, separate rooms and made any phone calls we wanted to make regarding the major life decision that would happen the following day. Both of us agreed that we were going to call our parents to let them know. I would call Beck, and we each had a few others that we would let know what was going on.

I felt so certain about everything that delivering the news to my family was easy. I told them we were getting married in a private ceremony in Vegas before heading to the lake house for a week.

My parents weren't happy at first, but I was so sure and easy-going about it, that they finally relaxed and agreed with me that everything would be all right. I explained rationally that I was happy with having things this way, and I was more than ready to be married to Wes. I believe the rebellious streak that led to acting prepared them for it because they quickly recovered, and by the end of the conversation were wishing us their best.

I took a deep breath, sitting on the edge of the bed after I talked to my family. I would shower and then go over to Wes's room to watch a little TV with him before coming back over here for bed.

I was thinking about everything. Thoughts flashed in my mind—everything from picturing our wedding, to picturing me snuggling with Wes on the couch.

I took a moment to pause and reflect before I jumped in the shower, and during those few seconds, I saw the screen of my phone light up. I glanced down to find that it was a text from my friend, Nadine. I opened it and stared down at it. I hadn't spoken to her in a long time, and I smiled as I stared at my screen to read her text.

Nadine:

Hey friend, I'm coming back to town for a women's leadership conference at Crossroads, and I thought maybe we could do lunch or coffee. It's been a while, so I don't think I've told you that I met someone! His name is Jacob, and I've been seeing him for a couple of months. Hope you are well, and I'll look forward to maybe grabbing a bite to eat next week. PS, did you ever go back and talk to that guy at the coffee shop?

Epilogue

A year later
The Academy Awards ~ An Afterparty

My feet ached, my back ached, and I had never fake smiled and sucked in my gut for so many hours in a row.

I was miserable….

…and it was absolutely glorious.

"I thought you had that one in the bag."

I heard someone talking to me from behind, but I didn't turn around. The statement applied to me since I had, indeed, lost an Oscar tonight, but I didn't want to assume, so I didn't turn.

Then I felt a tap on my shoulder.

"I thought the award was yours tonight," I heard her repeat, this time closer to my ear. I turned to find a woman staring at me. She smiled. "Lila Morgan?"

Wes and I had been married for a year, and my legal name was now Lila Quinn, but everyone knew me as Lila Morgan from the movie, and that was what my stage name remained.

"Yes," I said.

"I'm Logan's wife, Rachael."

"Oh, my goodness, it's so nice to meet you. You have a beautiful home."

The after party was at the home of one Logan Ritchie, who as we all know, was a longstanding Hollywood heartthrob with a couple of Oscars of his own.

"We were happy to get the invitation to be here," I continued.

"Oh, we were excited when you said you could make it. We don't do this every year, but Logan was presenting tonight, so we thought we'd get into the spirit."

"He did a good job," I said. "I've been a fan for a long time, so like I said, I was really happy to get your invitation. I didn't know Ryder was friends with Logan but when he mentioned coming over here, Wes and I both knew it was the party we wanted to come to. Your invitations were so cute, too. Did you say your name was Rachael?"

"Yes. Rachael Ritchie. And really, you did such a great job in that movie. I had no idea you were playing two roles. Christine was just so... tormented."

"Thank you," I said. I looked her in the eyes and I could tell she was just a real person—someone I liked instantly. "Susan deserved it tonight. I was glad to see her win. And, as much as I wanted it, I was really nervous at the thought of going up there. This is all so new to me that, I was almost praying *against* winning when he opened the envelope. Is that terrible to admit? I would've loved to have won, don't get me wrong, I was petrified."

"I totally get it. Show business is not for the faint of heart, but ultimately you would've just smiled and gone up there and said a few words just like everyone else."

"I know," I said. I took a breath and smiled at her. "I'll get 'em next time."

She grinned back and reached down for my hand. "I believe it," she said. "Let it be noted that I'm a fan."

"Thank you for being so sweet," I said. "That means a lot. I'm a big fan of your husband's."

"Thank you," she said. "We're very blessed." "What are you working on now?" she asked, still holding my hand.

"We're about to start the second season of Red Wall."

"Is that the book by Neil Britton?"

I nodded.

"Did you star in the first season?" she asked.

I nodded.

"Is it out yet?"

I shook my head. "No, it's coming out next month."

"Do you have fun working on it?"

"I love it," I said. "The costumes are intense. I have to sit through an hour-and-a-half of makeup every day, but it's so worth it. I think your husband might be looking for you," I added as I caught sight of Logan Ritchie walking across the next room as if he was searching for something.

Rachael glanced that way and then back at me. "I better go see what he needs. Please don't take off before we get to talk again."

"I won't," I promised, and we hugged before parting ways.

There were maybe a hundred people at the party. Logan had a big house, so I wasn't sure exactly how many. I had been separated from Wes for the last half-hour while I talked with Naomi Goldstein, daughter of Sal Goldstein, one of the best film directors in the world. Naomi was making a name for herself as a director, and she introduced herself to me. We got along great, and I could see myself working with her in the future.

I had been on my way back to my husband when I ran into Logan's wife. He was in the living room, talking to Ryder. He had his back turned to me.

Ryder saw me coming and pointed my way, and just like that, Wes turned and came toward me. Ryder remained behind him, talking with two other people. Everyone was engaged in their own conversation. Music and murmurs happened all around us.

I was still in the same dress I had worn to the Oscars, though I had traded my heels for a pair of Converse that were the same color.

Wes and I converged near a wall in Logan's living room. He had on a tux, but he had long before taken off his jacket and vest. His sleeves were rolled, his tie was off, and his shirt had the first two buttons undone. I felt a surge of excitement at the sight of him.

He pulled me into his arms and I went to him, holding onto him and staring up adoringly. He was a rockstar, and he had been my actual rock through all of this. He was writing his next project, but money had started to come in from the movie and from his investments, so he wasn't in a huge hurry to start his next film. For now, he traveled with me and worked from wherever I was working.

I stared at his neck, near the underside of his jaw, feeling like I wanted to lean in and kiss him.

"What did Naomi say?" he asked.

I could see his Adam's apple move when he spoke, and his voice rumbled low in his chest. Maybe it was the adrenaline after such a great night, maybe it was that I hadn't seen him in the last few minutes and I missed him, but either way, I felt like I couldn't get close enough to Wes. I couldn't wait till we were alone in the car.

"I'll be ready to get back to the hotel before too long," I said.

"Oh, will you?" he asked pulling me closer.

"Yes, I will. I'm ready whenever."

"How did it go with Naomi?"

"We get along so well," I said. "I could really see myself working with her. She asked me what I had on my books, and I told her I was working until

November. She seemed interested, though. We definitely got along. I also met Logan Ritchie's wife. She was so sweet, too. I'm really glad we came to this one."

I held onto Wes's mid-section and stared into his dark brown eyes. He was cool and easy, and oh so handsome. He was the indie director that broke onto the Hollywood scene on his first try. I was proud of him.

"I love you," I said.

Wes leaned down to speak near my ear. "I love you, too. And you might need to wait a year to put something on your books," he added before kissing me on the cheek.

"Why?"

"Because… you never know… you might have to take maternity leave."

Wes was the one who had been leaning toward waiting to have children. I had been ready to try for a baby for months. I knew I could finish my current project and schedule a break if we conceived. I had talked to him about it, but we hadn't started trying. I felt a wave of emotion and anticipation wash over me when he said that. I pulled him closer. Then I caught sight of Ryder, waving at me.

"Ryder's calling us over there, my love, but I'd *really* love to talk more about this later."

He grinned at me, a look of challenge. "We will," he said.

The End
(till book 3)

Thanks to my team ~ Chris, Coda, Jan, Glenda, and Yvette